"I . . ." He paused and drew in a deep breath.

Laura waited, her heart in her throat. He was going to kiss her. She could feel it all the way through her.

He lowered his head and cupped her chin, lifting her face to his. The look in his eyes simmered with desire, and his voice whispered to her with an almost haunting sadness.

"I want you, Laura." His thumb gently stroked the edge of her mouth. "I know it's too soon. I know all the reasons you think it couldn't work. But I can't help the way I feel. I don't want to say good-night to you. I don't want to go to my room and sleep alone."

She hadn't realized how much she wanted him until she tried to say no. She stood there, surrounded by him, her eyes wide and eloquent with the agony of her decision.

He didn't move. The muscles of his clenched jaw stood out, and slowly the hand that held her chin dropped to his side.

"I had to ask," he said quietly. "If you change your mind, you know where my room is."

Dear Reader,

The name Silhouette **Special Edition** represents a commitment—a commitment to bring you six sensitive, substantial novels every month, each offering a stimulating blend of deep emotions and high romance.

This month, be sure to savor Curtiss Ann Matlock's long-awaited *Love Finds Yancey Cordell* (#601). And don't miss Patricia Coughlin's unforgettable *The Spirit Is Willing* (#602), a deliciously different novel destined to become a classic. Four more stellar authors—Tracy Sinclair, Debbie Macomber, Ada Steward and Jessica St. James—complete the month's offerings with all the excitement, depth, vividness and warmth you've come to expect from Silhouette **Special Edition**.

Deeply emotional, richly romantic, infinitely rewarding—that's the Silhouette **Special Edition** experience. Come share it with us—six times a month!

From all the authors and editors of Silhouette **Special Edition**,

Best wishes,

Leslie Kazanjian
Senior Editor

ADA STEWARD
Galahad's Bride

Silhouette Special Edition

Published by Silhouette Books New York

America's Publisher of Contemporary Romance

SILHOUETTE BOOKS
300 East 42nd St., New York, N.Y. 10017

ISBN: 0-373-09604-6

First Silhouette Books printing June 1990

Printed in the U.S.A.

Books by Ada Steward

Silhouette Special Edition

This Cherished Land #227
Love's Haunting Refrain #289
Misty Mornings, Magic Nights #319
A Walk In Paradise #343
Galahad's Bride #604

ADA STEWARD

began writing a novel at the tender age of twelve, when romance and romantic fiction were the farthest things from her mind. As a preteen, she favored the fast-paced action of Westerns, war stories, even science fiction. As she matured, however, she realized that what fascinated her most in life *and* in writing were people, and she turned her attention more fully to character. Since she was drawn to travel, the particular flavor and history of settings also became important. Romantic fiction provided the perfect opportunity to combine the richness of place with the drama of people and possibilities. An Oklahoma resident, Ada Steward parcels most of her time into working, writing, traveling and exercising.

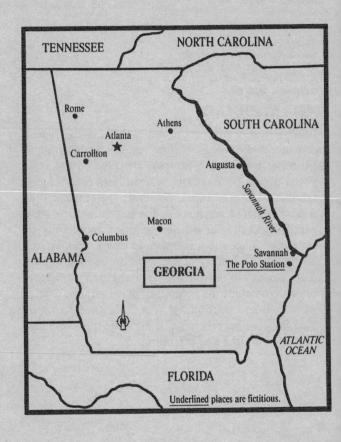

TENNESSEE

NORTH CAROLINA

Rome

Athens

SOUTH CAROLINA

Atlanta

Carrollton

Augusta

Savannah River

Macon

Columbus

Savannah
The Polo Station

ALABAMA

GEORGIA

ATLANTIC
OCEAN

FLORIDA

Underlined places are fictitious.

Chapter One

The lush scent of roses drifted upward on moist morning air as Laura Warner opened the French door wider and stepped out onto her bedroom balcony. Closing her eyes against the sudden bright light, she lifted her arms over her head and reached high in a long, luxurious stretch.

The soft, loose sleeves of her robe slid down her arms and draped around her shoulders as she twisted first one way then the other, relishing the taut pull of the muscles that ran across her stomach and up the sides of her rib cage. Any movement felt good after sitting for so long, even if that movement was just a stretch.

She had been awake since before daybreak, unable to sleep. "Ugh." With a mock shudder, she grimaced and dropped her arms to her sides. It was time to face the truth. She had been awake since daybreak, sitting in her room, not unable to sleep but postponing the inevitable.

Wincing at that thought, Laura turned slowly toward the sun and stood quietly for a moment. The early morning rays slanted soft and warm on her face as she absorbed the promise of the day, wishing that somewhere within that shining promise she could find an acceptable answer to her dilemma.

As she stood there, the high, impatient whinny of a horse drifted to her. It was echoed by another's strident call. Even softened by distance, the sounds tugged sharply at her conscience, and suddenly the balcony and the morning's gentle awakening were no longer a refuge from the battle she waged within herself.

Like a bad dream the nagging anxiety that haunted her was back. Turning away, Laura stepped through the open French door into the quiet womb of her bedroom. Next to the massive four-poster bed that was a Warner heirloom was the round table where she had spent most of the morning sitting and thinking while she had arranged and rearranged the scattered pieces of an old jigsaw puzzle.

She should be dressed. She should be downstairs. She should . . . The halfhearted scolding died silently as she stared at the table and the puzzle pieces without seeing them.

She should talk to her father. That's what she should do, she reluctantly told herself for what must be the hundredth time that morning. And for the hundredth time she tried to ignore the thought.

With a sigh that sounded more like a groan, she settled once more into the rose satin chair beside the chintz-covered table. Her restless fingers wandered over the familiar puzzle pieces, plucking up one and laying it down again, then moving to another only to discard it as quickly.

Her eyes searched the sliver of nature visible through the open balcony door, drawn there again and again as if an answer lay hidden somewhere within the subtle autumn shades, while her hands continued their blind repetitions. She had to tell him soon.

"Miss Laura?"

Laura's heart leaped into her throat as she turned toward the soft voice and found Etta Henderson standing just inside the bedroom door. Almost as embarrassed as she was startled, she put a calming hand over the jumping pulse at the base of her throat and said hi.

Etta extended the breakfast tray she held in front of her and started across the room with a look of determined cheeriness. "When you didn't come down, I decided I would come up. Why don't we eat outside this morning? Looks like it's going to be a beautiful day until the rain hits."

Laura hastily rose to intercept the older woman and gently took the tray. "I'll get it. I didn't know it was going to rain," she said, stepping through the balcony doors and setting the tray on a glass-topped dining table. Then she fixed a thoughtful frown on the woman who had been the Warners' housekeeper and cook, and Laura's friend and confidante from earliest memory. "Is your arthritis acting up again this morning?"

With a dismissing shrug of her shoulders, Etta eased herself into a chair and smiled ruefully. "A bit."

Laura shook her head and sank into the chair opposite Etta's. "Now I'm going to feel bad about you climbing those stairs." She was almost, but not quite, teasing, and her knees couldn't help aching just a little at the thought.

But Etta merely laughed, a deep, hearty laugh that never failed to lift the spirits of anyone who heard it, and she leaned across the table to pat Laura's hand. "I've got arthritis, honey. I'm not crippled. When it hurts too much for me to climb those stairs, I'll just quit climbing them."

Still, Laura couldn't stop the guilty feelings that seemed to be multiplying inside her like eager amoebas. She couldn't remember when she'd had a worse morning. "I still should have gone down sooner," she mumbled more to herself than to Etta.

"Quit fretting, child." Etta's tight brown and gray curls bobbed as she nodded toward Laura's bedroom and smoothly changed the subject. "I couldn't help noticing you've got that puzzle out again. It looks like you've been up for a while now."

"I have been." Laura slowly lifted her head until her pale green eyes peered out through a soft tumble of long, dark gold waves. She didn't entirely trust the sudden shift in the conversation.

Etta busied herself for a moment pouring coffee for the two of them. When Laura took the cup she offered, Etta caught her gaze and held it. "Is it something you'd want to talk about?"

Laura started to answer. Then she shook her head and gulped a mouthful of hot coffee instead.

But the distracting scald of the coffee didn't stop her troubled thoughts. She *needed* to talk to someone, whether she wanted to or not. And if she couldn't talk to Etta, she knew she would never be able to talk to Max. But those first few words were so hard.

"You know," Etta said with the softness of old memories, "I can remember when you were a little girl." She nodded gently and smiled while she took the covers off the plates on the tray. The plate with the smaller portions she set in front of Laura and continued, "The hours you used to spend on your jigsaw puzzles. Every time you had a problem, you'd take that puzzle..." She tilted her head toward the bedroom. "That same one you're working on now. And you'd go off by yourself and start fitting those little pieces together. I don't know if you've ever finished the puzzle, but you've always found an answer to whatever was bothering you. I expect you'll find your answer this time, too." She pointed her fork at Laura's plate. "Go on, dear. Eat. Starvation won't make your problem go away any faster."

Needing no more urging, Laura put aside her worries for the moment and eagerly lost herself in the scrambled eggs, hash browns and biscuits generously covered with sausage gravy.

The food was heaven, a balm for the most grievous hurt. No trouble was serious enough to kill an appetite that was confronted with one of Etta's meals. Her pride in her cooking was Etta Henderson's only vanity, and feeding others was her greatest joy.

She beamed as she watched Laura eat. Then she asked a little too casually, "Did you hear the arrival last night?"

Caught with a full mouth, Laura stared with round, questioning eyes as she chewed and carefully swallowed. She washed the delicious mouthful down with coffee that was every bit as good and asked, "Arrival?"

"A guest of your father's. He got in late last night." A soft flush crept upward over Etta's face until it glowed from her eyes as if a light had been switched on inside. "Has quite a healthy appetite, too. And such a gentleman. Didn't want to bother me last night, so he wouldn't eat." Her smile grew wider. "But he had *three* helpings for breakfast."

Seeing the pride and approval that shone so starkly from the other woman's face, Laura regretted not asking for a few more second helpings over the years. For a woman who lived to feed people, Etta must find the Warner household pretty disappointing now that Max had been put on a strict diet by his doctor.

As it did so often these days, the thought of her father brought a thin frown to Laura's brow. "You know, it's funny that Dad didn't mention he was expecting a visitor."

"Is it?" Etta leaned back and fixed Laura with a flat, no-nonsense look. "I'd say it sounds pretty much like your dad to me."

As she absorbed the truth of Etta's remark, Laura slowly relaxed her furrowed brow. "Yeah, I guess you're right," she said grudgingly. "It really does sound *just* like him." It was a sad but true fact that she knew very little about her father, his life or his friends anymore.

Laura set her empty plate on the tray and poured herself another half cup of coffee. Sitting back in her chair with the coffee cup cradled in her hands, she asked, "Who is he, this guest? A real friend or just a business friend?"

"Houston came for a polo clinic a couple of years ago," Etta answered quietly while she watched Laura for a reaction. "Since then he's been back two or three times a year, mainly just to visit. So I guess that would make him a real friend."

Laura nodded, frowning again, and rolled her cup between her hands. It wasn't normal for her to resent someone she had never met, but she couldn't help thinking how much harder it was going to be to talk to Max now that he had a houseguest, especially someone from his beloved world of polo.

Adrift in her own troubled world, Laura stared hard at the dark, swirling liquid in the cup she held. By the oily look of it, she could tell the coffee would soon be too cool to drink. "I guess we must have just missed each other last spring, this Houston person and I," she said finally. "I didn't realize Dad ever had any of the polo people stay in the main house."

"Houston's one of the few who have. Now that you're back for good, I guess you'll be meeting more of your father's friends." At the thought, a warm smile began to spread across Etta's face, then faded away when she saw the abrupt transformation in Laura's expression.

Now that you're back for good... The words replayed in Laura's head while she set her cup down and pushed herself away from the table. Shaken, she rose and walked blindly to the balcony railing.

Her eyes were locked on the trees in the distance, but she saw only the turmoil inside her mind. She had avoided the inevitable for too long already. Whether or not the words came easily, she was going to have to tell somebody about her change of plans. It just wasn't right to keep the news a secret any longer, especially not from Etta.

"What is it, Laura?" The older woman's voice was suddenly shaky, as if she'd just had the breath knocked out of her. "For days now you've been getting quieter and quieter." Etta hesitated and almost drew back. Then with a heavy sigh she asked, "Things haven't worked out the way you'd hoped, have they?"

Laura shook her head sadly and slowly turned. "No," she said barely above a whisper. "No, they haven't."

"You've just got to give him time, honey."

The plea in Etta's voice hurt more than Laura would have imagined it could. Burning tears gathered at the base of her throat, but she swallowed hard and held them there.

"It's been six months, Etta. And it's worse now than it's ever been." Her words sounded deep and gruff as they forced their way past the burning lump in her throat. "I've just been kidding myself. Dad's never going to change."

Etta's only reply was, "You're leaving." It wasn't a question. It was a statement, and it was leaden with grief.

But for Laura, hearing the words said aloud finally was a strange relief, and she couldn't help smiling softly when she looked into Etta's troubled hazel eyes. Wondering at her own unexpected reaction, she gazed lovingly over the deep lines of age and worry and toil that were etched into the older woman's face, fixing the image in her mind. And instead of the sadness she had expected to feel, Laura felt only happiness and relief, relief that her news wasn't nearly as bad as Etta seemed to expect.

"I'm not leaving right away," she said gently, and sat again. "And I'm not going far." The nervous tension that had been knotted inside Laura for days finally began to relax. "I'm opening a business in Savannah. I have an appointment with a realtor this afternoon."

"Savannah." Etta laughed aloud. "Why, that's not so far." Her smile beamed once again, and she leaned forward eagerly to warm Laura's lukewarm coffee with another half cup. "That's barely an hour's drive. What kind of business is it, darlin'?"

"Well," Laura said slowly, vacillating between excitement and a fresh surge of uncertainty that threatened to overcome her, "I want to combine a gourmet coffee shop with a tearoom. On River Street."

Etta took a sip of coffee while she let Laura's words hang in the air a little longer than was comfortable. Replacing her cup with great care in its saucer, she asked, "That's going to be awfully expensive, isn't it?"

The muscles along Laura's spine tightened again. "The initial outlay will be fairly staggering," she acknowledged. A simple yes would have been sufficient, but bigger words and longer sentences seemed to hold reality a little farther away.

"I didn't know you had that kind of money, sugar."

Laura took a deep breath and tried to relax. "I'm not sure I do," she said finally.

"Have you talked to Max?"

Everything Laura had spent the morning trying to control came rushing in on her with a suddenness that left her reeling. A confusion of raw emotion, self-doubt and anxieties crashed down around her until she found herself clutching the arms of her chair to keep from bolting to her feet to pace the confines of the balcony.

Etta's eyes slowly widened. "Oh," she said softly. Then, with a bluntness that cut to the bone, Etta continued, "It's because of Max that you're leaving in the first place. And you'd eat live red ants before you'd ask him for any money." She ticked off the statements on her fingers, then lifted one brow and regarded Laura carefully. "Does that about cover it?"

Laura drew in another long, deep breath and gripped the arms of her chair even tighter. "That about covers it," she said, expelling the words in a constricted sigh.

Her voice sounded as hollow as she felt, and this time there was no sense of relief in having the situation stated aloud for her. Max was her father. She loved him, probably too much. And she would gladly give everything she had if it would make him love her, too.

But it wouldn't. Nothing she had tried in the past fourteen years had accomplished that miracle, and living day in and day out with his indifference had become more than she was willing to bear.

"When are you planning to tell him?" Etta asked quietly.

Glad to dismiss her unhappy thoughts, Laura lifted her gaze to Etta and almost smiled. "Any day now. If

I like this property I'm looking at this afternoon, I won't be able to put it off much longer."

"I wish it didn't have to be this way." Etta reached across the table to give her hand an encouraging squeeze. "Good luck, sweetheart."

Taking a deep breath, Laura smothered the hot sting of fresh tears and managed to reward Etta with a radiant, and only slightly forced, smile. "So tell me, what does our houseguest look like? Just in case I bump into him today."

"A tall, slim, good-looking Texan," Etta said with genuine feeling.

Laura laughed, sliding quickly into a better mood. "Is there any other kind?"

"Not if you're talking to a Texan." Etta laughed with her and began to arrange their empty plates on the tray. "Well, I wish I could stay here all day, honey, but I've got work to do."

"Let me guess," Laura teased. "Will a certain Texan be included at lunch?"

Etta glanced up and winked to cover the happy blush that stained her cheeks. "With an appetite that does the state proud," she said.

Still chuckling, Laura gently forced Etta's hands from the tray. "Leave it. I'll bring it when I come down." She stood. "If I'm going to get a ride in before meeting this paragon at lunch, I'd better hurry."

"I can take the tray," Etta argued as Laura herded her toward the door.

"So can I," she said calmly, and ushered Etta into the hallway. "Now go. I have things to do."

"You won't forget the tray?"

"I won't forget the tray."

An hour later, more than a mile from the house, and on horseback, Laura remembered the tray, neatly stacked, sitting in the sun on the balcony. "Oh, no," she groaned in remorse, then hurriedly ducked one more low-hanging branch that her horse stubbornly refused to avoid. She'd find a way to apologize to Etta later. First she had to concentrate on living through this ride.

"Thanks a lot, Stubby," she muttered when she could sit upright in the saddle again. The short roan gelding was normally a steady, untemperamental mount, but even he had his moody days, and this was turning out to be one of them. Every time Laura had allowed her mind to wander, the gelding had brought her attention back with a new act of rebellion.

In a thirty-minute ride that had begun to seem like an eternity, he had already brushed her against a fence, shied violently when a bird had flown at his side and, finally, tried repeatedly to decapitate her with tree limbs.

Determined to take command, Laura tightened the grip of her legs and readjusted her hold on the reins. With a hard dig of her heel into the horse's side and with steady leg pressure, she firmly guided him out of the trees and onto the bridle path. Keeping the momentum, she lifted out of the saddle, heels down in the stirrups.

"Come on, Stub, old boy," she urged. Her hands at his neck, she pushed him on, and with no further encouragement, the stocky gelding broke into a smooth trot.

Posting in rhythm with the horse's stride, Laura concentrated on enjoying the exhilarating union. All too soon her legs would tire, her mind would wander and she would lose her balance, causing the gelding to break his trot.

But for the moment they moved in unison through a green, sun-dappled corridor in the lush Georgia wood. A gentle breeze grazed the glistening surfaces of horse and rider alike. The air's soft caress soothed the heated exertion of working muscles. And those few, brief moments were worth all the rest.

Laura breathed deeply of the sultry forest air and tried not to notice the inevitable weakening of her legs. For some, riding was a natural and effortless sport. But she was a land animal, and riding, for her, was an aerial act—a hard-fought and fleetingly won battle of balance atop a massive, marginally cooperative and stubbornly independent animal. It was a battle that she returned to again and again, however, and one that in spite of everything she never ceased to enjoy.

Ahead, sunlight bathed an opening in the bridle path, and Laura urged Stubby on as she recognized the point where a second straighter trail led from a clearing, through a smaller wooded patch and across a pasture before it ended at the stables. It was a trail she used when, like today, she was rushed for time.

When her horse broke from the shadowed path and into the sun-drenched clearing, Laura saw in an unfocused flash that it contained another horse and its dismounted rider. Then, in one stride, Stubby changed direction, toward the other horse, while Laura continued straight ahead.

She had only the briefest space of a heartbeat to tuck her shoulder under her and prepare to roll as her father had taught her. She might have a dislocated shoulder, he had said again and again, but she wouldn't have a broken neck. She repeated the words to herself just before she hit the ground with a bone-shaking thud and slid two feet into the base of a tree.

The air went out of her in a rush, and time seemed to stand still as a dazzling array of shooting stars crossed the black firmament of her mind. Caught by the roaring wind that swept over the landscape, the stars swirled and circled and swooped, ending in great, brilliant bursts of white light that arced through the blackness.

Dazed, Laura watched the display with awe. Falling off her horse was nothing new. And she'd knocked herself silly more than once. But the phrase "seeing stars" had never had quite such a meaning before.

"Oh-h." Over the chiming of bells that rang sharply inside her head, she heard a groan. It was weak and far away. And with it there was something else. Something . . .

"Oh-h." The groan was louder and seemed to echo inside her. The other sound was deep, like a growl, growing softer as it mingled with the incessant ringing.

"Awyawright?"

Laura turned her head toward the insistent baritone rumble and began to draw a breath to answer, but nothing happened. There was no air. And something the size of an elephant seemed to be sitting on her chest.

She tried to struggle, but her arms could have belonged to anyone. She couldn't feel them. Her legs were lifeless weights that remained rooted to the ground.

And she couldn't *breathe*. Panic swept through her with the gathering speed of a runaway train plunging down a mountainside. Laura opened her mouth and tried to gasp, but nothing happened.

The man spoke again, and his words buzzed senselessly around her. Then something touched her arm, and she savagely flung it off as she fought for air to fill her empty lungs.

For seconds that felt like hours there was nothing but a burning, aching void inside her. Then, just as she was sure she was moments from dying, the viselike grip of her chest loosened. As quickly as it had come, the panic receded, and Laura lay limp on the grass, drawing in lungful after lungful of precious air.

"... breath knocked out of you. I wasn't sure for a minute if you were going to be all right."

He was still there. Right beside her. Laura rolled her head toward the sound of his voice and slowly focused on a pair of dusty, battered cowboy boots a few feet away.

"That was quite a tumble you took."

The folksy warmth of his deep voice lingered in the air as Laura's gaze moved up from the man's boots past the stovepipe hem of his well-worn jeans. She liked the sound of his voice. Pleasant sensations mingled with the dull ache that had begun in her head and was rapidly moving through her body.

"Glad you liked it," she croaked in rusty tones.

He laughed, and his whole body seemed to relax. "Think anything's broken?"

Laura wiggled one foot and slowly drew the other leg up, knee bent skyward, while her eyes moved up over the faded knees of his skintight jeans. "Everything seems to be working,'' she said in a more normal voice.

"Glad to hear it. That was a dandy little tuck and roll you did. But you're still gonna be one big bruise tomorrow.''

She smiled at the Texas drawl that coated his words like honey on a hot afternoon. Then she drew in a long, lazy breath and continued her slow, visual stroll up the stranger's body. By the time she reached his belt buckle, she felt she knew him well enough to call him by his first name.

Ignoring her silence, he went on, "You had me kind of scared for a minute there, ya know.''

He knelt beside her, and without warning Laura found herself staring into his concerned blue eyes. Curly brown hair slipped from under his cowboy hat as he thumbed it back from his face, and her lingering, impersonal inspection of him came to a jolting halt.

"Uh, I'm fine,'' she said slowly, wanting to draw away and move nearer at the same time. "Really.''

His smile was a slow, sweet echo of his drawl, and Laura's stomach fluttered alarmingly. "I caught your horse for you,'' he said, and gestured across the clearing. "He's with mine.''

"Horse?'' Laura echoed.

His smile widened to display straight, white teeth against golden tan skin. "You know. The big brown thing you rode in on.''

Suddenly remembering Stubby, her fall and the killer ride home, Laura closed her eyes and released a long, low groan of despair.

"Hey, hold on," his deep baritone coaxed. "You were doing so well. Don't pass out now."

A strong, callused hand that was amazingly gentle in its touch brushed her hair from her brow, and Laura's eyes popped instantly open.

His face was only inches from hers, and she couldn't help the gasp that escaped her. His features were too bold to be perfect, especially when viewed so close, but they were clean and strong and oh, so male—especially when viewed closely.

"Do you hurt?" he asked, stroking her cheek with a touch that was feather light and dizzyingly intimate.

Laura shook her head and stared into eyes that were the deep, dazzling blue of sapphires.

"Are you dizzy?" he asked, leaning even nearer.

She drew in an uneven breath and felt the closeness of the arm that stretched across her to the ground on the other side, bracing him as he leaned over her. Directly above was a shoulder that jutted broad and straight as a slab of granite.

"I'm fine," she said, but even to her own ears she sounded weak to the point of fainting.

With the speed of a man to whom thought and action were obviously one, he withdrew. The next instant she felt his hands, warm and caressing, on her leg. His strong fingers gripped either side of her calf above her boot and quickly moved upward, leaving a trail of tantalized nerve endings that went straight to the pit of her stomach.

By the time the probing fingers reached her knee, Laura had come out of her stupor and bolted upright. "What are you doing..."

Her aroused indignation evaporated in a swirl of green landscape that turned pale blue as she crumpled backward. Quick hands caught her shoulders just before she crashed to the ground a second time.

"You shouldn't sit up so fast." Behind the stern warning was a tone of genuine concern as he settled himself against the tree behind her and cradled Laura's head in his lap.

"Now you tell me," she murmured without opening her eyes.

"And I was just checking for broken bones." His tone carried a gentle reprimand.

"You startled me." Her voice was growing stronger, aided by a slight embarrassment at the lightning speed of her reaction. She had seen her father check a fallen rider in just the same way a hundred times. She should have known what he was doing.

"Well, at least I know nothing's broken," he said, humor creeping into his voice. "Nobody who's really hurt could move that fast."

"You startled me," she repeated.

"So you said." His fingers slid through her hair, smoothing it away from her face. He lifted a lock and watched the sunlight play over the golden strands as they slipped through his fingers. "Are you feeling better?" he asked softly.

Laura opened her eyes to a world that stood still. No black dots danced in front of her eyes. No white stars burst in the heavens.

She was almost disappointed. She had begun to enjoy the feel of his fingers in her hair and the hard muscles of his thighs against the back of her neck. "Much better," she said without enthusiasm.

"You know, your horse looks sort of familiar. It's from Max Warner's stable, isn't it?"

She nodded, wishing she could escape what came next. People who had met Max recently never seemed to know he had a family. She always hated the look of surprise that sprang into their eyes, and the sudden appraisal that followed when they learned she was his daughter. She would especially hate to see those things in this man's eyes.

Oh, well. She shrugged and took a deep breath. "Yours is, too, isn't it?" she asked, carefully keeping her gaze on the trees straight ahead and trying not to enjoy it too much as he began to stroke her temples in a soothing, circular massage.

"Yeah. I'm staying with Max for a few days. Are you a friend of his, or a student?"

The touch of his hands could do nothing to ease the old, familiar mingling of pride and dread that curled around her heart. Laura had to push her words past the sudden catch in her throat. "I'm his daughter."

The thigh under her head tensed for a moment, and Laura closed her eyes against her slowly rising pain. She wouldn't look at his face. No matter what, she wouldn't look at his face.

"Well," he said at length. "That's a surprise."

"It always seems to be." She regretted the cold sound of her voice, but it matched the icy chill inside her.

She sat up suddenly, remembering too late the dizziness that had overcome her before. But this time nothing happened except that the hand that was entangled in her hair went with her.

"Whoa. What did I say?" He made no attempt to remove his hand from her hair. Instead, he leaned forward until his chest brushed against her back. "I don't mean to pry," he said softly at her shoulder, "but do I detect a sensitive issue here?"

She felt like a coiled spring, and the heat of his body so close to hers did nothing to melt the cold hurt inside her. "What would make you think that?"

"Maybe the fact that I've known Max Warner for three years and never heard him say the word 'daughter.'"

His fingers slid through her hair to the tensed muscles of her neck. Moving in slow, gentle circles, his fingertips soothed while his words probed. "Or maybe it was the way you bolted upright just a second ago. A person doesn't have to be psychic to read body language like that."

Laura's head tilted back. Her breath rushed out in a hard sigh as she stared at the gathering clouds in the blue sky. He was right, of course. And the urge to confide in this strangely compelling man grew stronger. There was something about him that made it so tempting for her to drop her guard, so easy to lean against his broad chest, be cradled in his strong arms and tell him everything that was inside her.

She lowered her gaze to the trees and straightened her spine, pulling imperceptibly away from his soothing presence. It was tempting, but not tempting enough to overcome half a lifetime of keeping the pain inside.

"I don't even know your name," she said softly.

"Houston." His hand slid from her neck, releasing the bond that tied them silently to each other. "Houston Carder."

The name went through her like a jolt of lightning, and she whirled, staring at him.

Houston's eyes locked onto hers while his brows crinkled in a puzzled frown. He reached out to trail his fingertips down her jaw. "Why do I get the feeling I just lost you?" he asked in a voice so quiet it was almost a whisper.

Laura's head sagged forward as she silently wished she could just wipe out the day. Nothing had gone right from the minute she had opened her eyes.

When she didn't answer, Houston said, "You've got to tell me what's going on here, because unless I was reading it all wrong, we were getting along great until you told me who you were and I told you who I am." He took her hands in his and leaned forward intently, compelling her to look at him. "It doesn't matter to me that you're Max's daughter, so why does my *name* bother you so much?"

Hearing it put that way, Laura couldn't help wondering if she might have overreacted just a bit. "You startled me," she said with a shrug, and longed to start over again with her head still in his lap.

"I seem to be doing a lot of that today." They looked at each other, and he began to smile slowly.

Making an effort to relax, Laura ran both hands through her hair, dragging the long strands from her face. "First, you have to understand that today has not been a good day for me so far," she said with an uneasy laugh.

"Maybe we can do something about that."

"Well, if you can think of something, please be my guest."

"Let's start with my name. What's the problem?"

She shook her head. "No problem. Etta and I were just discussing you this morning."

"Ah, Etta." At the sound of her name a satisfied smile lit his face.

"She's a fan of yours, too."

"So you'd heard of me. That explains surprise, maybe, but not shock and dismay."

She shrugged again, unable and unwilling to discuss her feelings of disappointment and betrayal when she realized who he was. So few men really wanted to discuss emotions. It was just her luck to find an enlightened male when she least wanted one. "You weren't what I was expecting," she hedged.

"Yeah," he said, and waited for her to continue.

"You're young. You're . . . nice."

Confused, he frowned. "What exactly did Etta tell you?" He watched her closely through narrowed eyes.

"That you were a friend of my father's. A polo buddy."

"That's it?"

Laura nodded.

The tension ebbed from his body, and the intensity of his gaze turned mischievous while the corners of his mouth curved slowly upward. "And from that you decided I'd be old and mean?"

She couldn't help laughing. "Well?" Her arms extended in a palms-up shrug.

"More like Max," he suggested helpfully.

She stared at the ground. "Maybe."

"So this is really about Max, and not about me at all."

Laura stood slowly, trying not to show the quaking she felt inside. With this man a little insight went a long way. She would have to be *very* careful what she said to him. Looking away, she dusted the seat of her pants.

"I guess we'd better start back soon. Dad doesn't like to wait lunch." She glanced toward Houston, who hadn't moved. "I wouldn't want to be blamed for making you a truant on your first day here."

Houston stood but made no move to cross the few feet to where she was. "Do you always change the subject when it's getting too close for comfort?"

The quiet tone of his question made it no less jarring. With a sigh redolent with strained patience, Laura looked at him. "Is it always so hard to get you to take a hint?"

"So I've been told," he said, rewarding her with another easy grin.

"Well, then, how's this? I don't want to discuss my father."

He nodded, still smiling. "Fine. You and I still friends?"

Relieved and once more relaxed in his company, she let out a soft laugh. "Sure. But I don't think Max is going to like this too well."

"He'll adjust."

"Things may get a little interesting while we're waiting for him to make this adjustment," she warned.

Houston took her hand and slowly walked beside her toward the horses. "Not to worry. Things are always more fun when they're a little interesting, don't you think?"

Chapter Two

Laura sipped the cup of hot tea she held in her hands and watched her father and Houston, deep in conversation across the room. Lunch *had* been interesting—not exactly fun, but interesting.

She didn't quite understand what the two men had in common besides polo, but the sense of camaraderie between them was unmistakable. As they leaned toward each other, almost whispering, she studied them.

This was the first time she had gotten a really good look at Houston from any distance. His shirt was a plain, plaid cotton, its sleeves rolled to his elbows. The forearms that were revealed were strong, as were the hands that moved restlessly as he spoke.

Where his shirt was tucked neatly into the waistband of his jeans, she could visualize the lean, rip-

pling stomach muscles underneath, as trim and solid
as the rest of him. His muscles had been shaped and
hardened outdoors, not in any weight room. His was
a working man's body.

Her father leaned forward suddenly, jabbing his
fingers in the air to make a point, and Laura realized
she had been openly staring. She settled deeper into
the cushions of the couch and raised her teacup. Over
the rim, feeling hidden while she sipped the tea, she
continued to watch the two who were so different and
yet so alike.

She could remember when her father had looked
very much like Houston. Fourteen years ago. Before
the accident.

By anyone's standards Max was a handsome man
still, with skin a deep, year-round tan and thick hair
that was almost pure white. His arms and chest were
even stronger and more heavily muscled now than they
had been . . . before. But his legs had grown thin and
wasted. And Max, who had once stood so tall and
proud, would never stand, or walk, or ride again.

Laura barely controlled a shudder at the waste, the
horrible waste, not just of his life, but of her life and
the lives of their whole family.

Since that day she had hated polo, hated the thought
of it, the sight of it, the sound of it. It had taken the
father she adored and given her a cold, unloving
stranger.

"Are you all right?"

The words were soft but close, and Laura jumped
as if a gun had gone off next to her. She jerked her
head up to see Houston standing barely a foot away.

Then, needing a moment to collect herself, she stared at the teacup that rattled against the saucer in her lap.

"You looked about a million miles away," Houston said as he sat beside her and took the cup and saucer out of her shaky hands. "We didn't mean to leave you sitting here all alone." The voice that had been solely for her rose slightly as he called, "Did we, Max?"

"What?"

Her father's gruff reply brought Laura back to the present. There was something about Houston that made it too easy for her to linger in memories of what it had once been like before her family had been split in two and the love banished from this big, empty house.

"I was just telling Laura that I was afraid we had been rude."

Houston took her hand tightly in his, and Laura steeled herself at the muffled sound of Max's wheelchair rolling toward them over the thick carpet.

"Rude?" Max demanded. "Were we being rude, Laura?"

She lifted her gaze to meet her father's. Once he had been her hero, her best friend. Now his penetrating hazel eyes seemed to challenge the world and her along with it.

"No, Daddy," she said quietly, trying not to let the broken pieces of her heart show. "No."

"Your father's trying to talk me into playing in a tournament while I'm here," Houston said cheerfully, as if the atmosphere in the room hadn't grown thick enough to cut with a knife.

In spite of herself, Laura stiffened.

"Laura doesn't approve of polo," Max said, not unkindly.

"Why not?" Houston asked. He looked from Max to Laura.

When she stared into his blue, blue eyes, she saw the pure passion of a dedicated player, and she wished she didn't like him quite so much.

"Me," Max answered for her, and slapped the arm of his wheelchair for emphasis.

"Any sport's dangerous, Laura," Houston argued gently. "I spent my high school years playing football and my college years riding the rodeo circuit on weekends." He laughed. "If you think a polo pony's dangerous, you ought to be flat on your back in an arena with a bull bearing down on you. Now that's dangerous."

When she just looked at him, he tried one more time. "Why, that fall you took this morning was as bad as any I've ever had."

"Fall?" Max rasped, leaning forward with a frown.

"Head first," Houston confirmed.

Laura looked at Max and saw him watching her while his frown disappeared and a slow smile grew in its stead. In that moment she felt the old camaraderie return, the joining of twin spirits that had been their special bond. And she'd have gladly fallen off a thousand horses if she could have held that moment forever.

"Slid into the trunk of a tree," Houston continued. His last word trailed off uncertainly, and he looked from father to daughter as Max began to chuckle and a slow smile spread across Laura's face.

"The girl's got heart," Max said proudly. "I'll give her that."

Laura relaxed against the back of the couch and laughed with him. Memories danced between them. Memories dearly cherished and as bright as if they were from yesterday, of a childhood that would never come again.

Houston stared at them both as if they were crazy. "She could have been hurt," he said with a stern frown.

Max nodded in happy agreement. "Worst rider I've ever seen." The smile that lingered as he looked at Laura was anything but cold. "But she never gives up."

Laura touched Houston's stiff arm soothingly. She hated to destroy the moment of reverie with her father, but she understood Houston's distress. "When I was a little girl," she said with a soft smile that asked him to understand, "Daddy taught me how to fall without hurting myself."

"Since it was obvious I could never get her to stop falling off," Max added. "She had a will of iron. And *no* coordination once she was off the ground."

Houston stared at her with a look that approached horror. He was trying to understand, but he had enough sense to realize that some people were meant to ride and some people weren't, and he couldn't comprehend a father who would encourage such foolishness. "Why don't you quit before you kill yourself?" he demanded.

Before Laura could answer, Max said, "I've never seen her give up. She may never be the best, but she'll never quit trying."

Laura looked into her father's eyes and knew their moment was gone. She could never bring herself to tell him so, but he had been the one to break her, finally. She was giving up. She was leaving.

Somewhere deep inside him Max still loved her. She knew he did, because in moments like these she could hear love's echo in his voice, see its shadow in his eyes. But the love itself remained hidden within him. And she just couldn't go on living with nothing more than the shadows and echoes of a love she used to feel so completely. She needed more—or nothing at all.

"Excuse me, Miss Laura," Etta said, coming quietly into the room. "But you have a phone call."

Relieved to get away before the conversation deteriorated once again into the uncomfortable fits and starts that had taken it through lunch, Laura rose. "I'll take the call in the foyer, Etta. Thank you." She nodded to her father then Houston. "You gentlemen go on without me."

When Laura closed the sitting room door behind her, Houston had the feeling she wouldn't be back, and he really couldn't blame her.

"You know, Max," he said, staring at the closed door, "I didn't realize you had a family."

"I forget it myself sometimes."

Houston turned to see Max wheeling himself away from the door. "I gathered that," he said, projecting his voice after the retreating man. "She had no idea who I was or why I was here."

"It's my place," Max growled without turning.

"And did this place mean anything to you when you were growing up here, Max?" Houston asked softly.

"Of course it did." Max pulled open the door of a compact refrigerator tucked into the corner of the room and took out a can of cold beer, then wheeled to face Houston. "Want one?"

Houston shrugged. "Might as well." As Max drew back his arm, Houston shouted, "Don't—" he released his breath in a disgusted huff and caught the beer in midair "—toss it," he finished in a monotone.

Max grinned wickedly and pulled out a can for himself.

"You realize what this is going to do when I open it," Houston said.

"You'll drip dry," Max answered without sympathy.

"I hope this room will."

"It's seen worse."

Houston grinned slowly, then began to laugh. How well he remembered some of the bon voyage parties Max had thrown at the end of his polo clinics. Houston had only attended one clinic, but he had come back for several of the parties. Max had built quite a reputation for his polo clinics, and there was heavy debate as to whether it was the quality of the teaching or the energy of the parties that held such an attraction. With a shrug, Houston popped the top of the can and endured the yeasty bath with a grin.

Taking a drink that was mostly foam, he said, "You know, I was trying to make a point a while ago."

"Yeah." Again Max flashed a wicked smile. "I thought I did a pretty good job of getting you off the track."

"Momentarily."

Max lifted his beer in a resigned salute. "Fire away."

"Well, don't you think maybe this place meant something to Laura when she was growing up here?"

"She hates polo."

"That doesn't mean she hates this place. Have you ever asked her?"

"No," Max snapped, "I haven't." He glowered over the top of his beer as he took a long drink. "Dammit, Houston," he said when he had swallowed and taken a few seconds to think, "I *hate* talking about this stuff."

"Well, I'm sorry, Max," Houston said, not sounding at all sorry. "But when you asked me to buy this place, I had no idea you had a daughter who might be expecting to inherit it."

"Daughters," Max corrected glumly.

"Daughters?"

"Laura and Lorene. Lorene's the oldest. She's married. I haven't seen her since she was sixteen, and I don't even get a Christmas card from her anymore."

Houston flinched inwardly and took another drink. He had thought Max's relationship with Laura was bad. After an uncomfortable cough, he said, "I didn't mean to pry."

"It's old news." Max balanced the can in his lap and wheeled himself across the room. "Point is, they don't care. Neither one of them."

Houston shook his head, unable to accept the easy answer. "Laura's living here. She wouldn't be here if she didn't care."

"She thought I was dying." Max spat out his words in short spurts, as if he begrudged saying them and wanted to get it over with. "I'm not. She'll be leaving again."

Houston shook his head in confusion this time. "I thought she lived here."

"You ever seen her here before?" Max demanded gruffly.

"No. But I haven't been here—"

"She thought I was dying," Max said again, interrupting. "I'm not, and when she figures that out, she'll leave again."

"And what if you're wrong?"

"I'm not."

Houston threw up his hands in frustration and clenched his teeth over an insult along the lines of "stubborn old goat." He took a long drink of the cold beer as he pulled the reins in hard on his temper.

"Okay, Max," he said calmly. "You know that I want this place. I love the farm. And with you staying on to manage the clinics and the training of the ponies, as a business it will continue to be as successful as it's ever been."

He watched to see that he had Max's full attention before he continued. "And I'll accept what you say about Lorene not caring. But..." He stopped again and could see Max's impatience building. "I won't finalize the deal until I know for myself that Laura won't be hurt by it."

"Dammit to hell!" Max exploded. He brought his hands down with a bang onto the arms of his wheelchair, and beer sloshed everywhere. "Who fell on their head this morning? Laura? Or you?"

"This land has been in your family for generations, Max," Houston continued in the same relentlessly calm voice. "And if you haven't talked to her about it, then you don't know *how* Laura feels."

"They'll get my money," Max snarled. "Or what's left of it, anyway."

"To a person who loves the land, money is no replacement. I wouldn't be looking for my own place if Dad's ranch didn't have to be split five ways."

"But she hates polo. And the Polo Station *is* polo. Without the income from that, this place wouldn't last a decade. The day of the gentleman farmer is dead, and Laura wouldn't have the money to keep this estate going if it couldn't pay its own way."

"So, why haven't you told her?" Houston persisted gently, aware that Max was quickly approaching one of his infamous rages.

"Aargh!" Max growled through clenched teeth as he pounded the arms of his chair.

Houston held up his hands innocently. "All I want to know is if my reason for being here is supposed to be a secret."

"Hell, yes!"

"I don't approve."

"Ah, Houston." Max let the words out in a long sigh. His shoulders drooped and his anger faded. "I always forget what a disgustingly decent man you are."

Houston smiled with all the congeniality he could muster. "Sorry."

"Give me some time, okay?" Max shifted his shoulders uncomfortably. "I'm just not ready to get into this with her right now."

"You *are* afraid of her reaction, aren't you?"

"I wouldn't call it afraid, exactly."

"Because you're not really sure she's planning to leave, are you?" Max looked at him sourly, and Houston continued, "And if she's not planning to leave, you don't want to do anything accidently that might drive her away. Am I right?"

"Do you know how much I hate to have you read my mind?"

Houston grinned. "I have a pretty good idea."

"Laura was always my favorite." Max's voice suddenly grew almost misty with reminiscence. "I tried not to let it show, but everybody knew. I expected more from her, and she never let me down."

"Things were a lot different before your accident, weren't they?"

"That's another story, for another time. And if it's just the same to you, son, I'm getting a little tired."

"Oh, sure," Houston answered, instantly contrite. Even though he was in a wheelchair, Max always seemed to be made of tempered steel. That was the image he projected, and Houston too often found himself forgetting that it wasn't always so. "How *are* you doing?" he asked. "And don't give me that bull you give other people."

"I'm tired. That pneumonia last spring took more out of me than I like to admit."

"Was it from that little cold you had the last time I was here?"

Max grinned sheepishly. "Yeah."

"I wish you'd have let me take you to the doctor when I wanted to."

"Yes, Mother."

"So, sue me. I like you, and I'd rather not see you die from something that stupid."

"But then Laura wouldn't be here," Max said simply.

"Ah, Max." Houston was amazed at the sincerity in Max's voice, and amazed that he was so amazed. Somehow, vulnerability was one of the last things he had expected to discover in Max Warner. But there it was. "You really love her, don't you? Why don't you tell her?" he almost whispered.

"I don't need her pity."

"Max!" In a flash, the gruff, snarling, thick-headed Max had returned, and Houston had to work hard to keep from shouting at him. "She's your daughter. She doesn't pity you. She loves you."

"Right. Excuse me. You've been here less than a day, but you've got all the answers." Max snapped his mouth shut and glared. Silence stretched as his anger slowly quieted, then he said, "The subject's closed, Houston. Okay?"

Recognizing a brick wall when he hit one, Houston lifted his hands in surrender and backed away. Max needed some space, and Houston needed a minute to squelch the frustration that boiled inside him.

The beer in the can he held was almost lukewarm, but Houston drank it anyway as he turned and walked to the row of windows at the front of the room.

From there he could see the gravel drive that circled in front of the house. The lane that led from the circle passed a long row of trees on its way to the stables and then on to the main road.

Along the way were more than a few sharp, blind curves, but it was a pretty drive and one that he always enjoyed. He always felt a sense of homecoming when he returned to the Polo Station.

"What was this place called before you changed the name, Max?"

"The Groves. There've been pecans here as long as there've been people."

Houston continued to stare out the window, trying to imagine what it must have been like to be a country gentleman on a plantation whose history was as old as the nation's. "Have the Warners always owned it?"

"Yep."

"You're crazy for selling it, Max."

"That may be, but if you won't take it, I'll find someone who will."

Houston couldn't help smiling. "Save your breath, you old horse trader. You know I'll never let that happen."

At the sound of the front door closing, Houston shifted his gaze to the broad porch to the right. He watched as a slender, leggy blonde in a tailored suit and high heels walked down the front steps, got into a low-slung red sports car and drove away, leaving scattered gravel and a drifting cloud of dust in her wake.

"Is there another woman here besides Laura?" he asked as the dust settled slowly in the still air.

"Etta. Somebody just drive off?"

Houston nodded without turning.

"Little red sports car?" Max asked.

"Yeah."

Max expelled his breath in a grumpy huff. "Drives that thing the way she rides a horse."

At that Houston turned. "Laura?"

"Who'd you think it was?"

"A woman."

Max shook his head. "I'm not even going to guess. I'll just let you tell me. What'd you think Laura was?"

Perplexed, Houston frowned. "A girl."

"Jailbait," Max suggested.

Houston frowned in disagreement. "Older than *that*." He crushed the empty beer can he still held and looked around for a trash can.

Max chuckled. "There's no in between with a female, Houston. They pass eighteen and go straight to woman."

Having found a trash can, Houston turned his attention to Max, but his thoughts were on Laura. "How old is she?"

"Well, I haven't kept up too good, but let's see... she was about twelve when... and that was... around twenty-six, I guess," Max finally said with a frown of concentration.

Houston whistled. "Damn, she looks *young* for twenty-six."

He'd been thinking of her as around twenty, tops. An age where he could appreciate her beauty without having to feel like a dirty old man, an age where he could feel drawn to her and protective of her, but an age where at thirty-three he had done too much living and she too little for him to let his feelings get serious. But twenty-six, that was different.

Houston shook his head and sat down. When he'd first seen her, she'd looked so little lying there in her T-shirt and jeans. Pretty, but little and pale. And once she'd gotten up and around, he'd tried hard not to notice the difference in the way she'd looked, and the way he'd felt.

Then at lunch, when she'd traded in her jeans for a
sundress, he couldn't help the way his eyes kept trac-
ing the smooth curve of her legs. But she'd still looked
so young and innocent with her fresh-scrubbed face
and her hair in a ponytail, still damp from the shower.
And it seemed that these days most girls over fourteen had a body any woman would be proud of, so
he'd just tried not to think about it.

But, damn, the woman he'd just seen leaving had
been...sophisticated. That was the only word he could
think of. And try as he might, he couldn't bring the
two images together into one woman.

Twenty-six. He gave it some thought and tried to get
used to the concept. With the care of a man tiptoeing
toward an elusive prey, he pictured Laura next to him
on the couch. The pale tan of her creamy, bare skin.
Her slender shoulders. Her hand, gentle and warm on
his arm. Her legs, with their graceful curves and delicately molded ankles. Her breasts, full and round
and . . .

Houston stood and walked to the window again. He
needed to move but didn't want to turn around for
fear Max would be watching. Somehow it just didn't
feel right, sitting in a man's house and getting aroused
by the thought of his daughter. He hadn't realized how
tightly he'd been controlling his feelings about Laura
until he suddenly discovered he didn't have to any
more.

Twenty-six. He shook his head again and slowly
smiled.

Laura parked just off Bay Street and walked across
the street, through a narrow park and down the steep,

cobblestone alleyway that was the beginning of Factor's Walk.

The sun had given up fighting the clouds, and the day had turned ominously overcast. A cool, damp breeze blew from the river, which was becoming visible as she neared the sharp curve in the drive. To her right she saw an L-shaped staircase cut into the sheer stone wall that towered above her. The stairs led from a park to the alleyway, and Laura made a mental note to take the staircase on her return trip and to leave her high heels at home the next time she came this way.

The round, uneven surfaces of the cobblestones underfoot were slick from centuries of use, and the deep gaps between the stones were treacherous. When she turned the corner at The Boar's Head Tavern and emerged onto an ordinary paved sidewalk she let out a sigh of relief and wiggled her toes gratefully inside her normally sensible pumps.

Lifting her eyes, Laura took in the view ahead of her. To one side was the Savannah River, empty except for a lone tugboat headed out to sea. Beside her, barely an arm's length away, were the shops and restaurants that lined River Street. The restored buildings, mostly cotton warehouses that predated the Civil War, housed apartments on the upper levels and, on the ground floors, anything anyone could dream of that might tempt a visitor to enter and purchase. And between the shops and the river was the brick-paved River Street itself, ancient and mysterious, alive with the ghosts of the cotton merchants and pirates who had once walked its length.

Laura hugged herself to ward off the chill that traveled up her spine. Maybe it was the mist that seemed to rise from the river and melt into the low-hanging clouds, or maybe it was the nearness of her own dreams, but she felt especially susceptible to the city's magic this afternoon.

Again she looked into the distance, and this time she saw a building farther down the street. A metal staircase led to a doorway on the second floor, and one story above that a wrought-iron balcony jutted out from three floor-to-ceiling windows. The staircase was rusty, and the three windows were coated with grime. The middle window was boarded at the top.

All in all, Laura had to admit it was a pretty discouraging sight. And yet, each time she saw the building, her heart filled with an unreasonable happiness. It was going to be hers. She just knew it. The second floor would house a gourmet tea and coffee shop, and the third floor would become a tearoom where she would serve breakfast and lunch during the week and extend the hours into the evening on the weekends. She probably wouldn't get rich, but she wouldn't go broke, either, and it was something she knew she would enjoy doing.

She glanced at her watch and hurried along the sidewalk. The realtor would be there any minute. As Laura walked closer, she concentrated on regaining her businesslike composure. Her hair had been smoothed into a French braid that tucked under at the nape of her neck. Her makeup was understated but painstaking. And her business suit was a retail Dior, a navy pinstripe that echoed her mother's lifelong advice to look expensive, not flashy.

A plump, motherly woman waited at the base of the staircase. Laura extended her hand. "I'm Laura Warner. And you're Mrs. Sanderson, I hope."

The other woman laughed and took her hand. "I am. It's a pleasure to meet you, Ms. Warner." She began to climb the stairs, talking to Laura over her shoulder. "I must say, I would have hoped for better weather. This place is going to look dreary enough as it is, I'm afraid. I did have a chance to get the electricity turned on after you called the other day. And I stopped by this morning to make sure there were light bulbs." She unlocked the door and pushed it open. With a cheerful smile, she stood aside for Laura to enter. "Well, here goes."

Stale, musty air drifted through the open door, and Laura felt her first flicker of uncertainty. "Yes," she answered with a wavering smile, "here goes." She went through the doorway and a few yards into the room before Mrs. Sanderson flipped on the overhead light, and Laura almost recoiled at the sight of the sagging ceiling, peeling wallpaper and debris-heaped floor.

"For a two-hundred-year-old building, it's in pretty good shape," Mrs. Sanderson said, drawing to a halt next to Laura. "The floors are dirty and scarred, but solid. The timber in the walls is sound. The brick walls are original and run from the basement to the roof. They're almost as good as new and serve as an excellent firebreak, just in case. It looks like hell, I know. But it's a good deal for the money."

Laura had no problem containing her excitement. It didn't take long for humidity to wreak havoc on waterfront buildings, and when a building was this old to start with, the havoc looked pretty bad. "Does it get any better?" she asked with a timidity that wasn't feigned.

"Not a bit," Mrs. Sanderson said bluntly. "If you don't want to go any farther, I understand."

"Oh, no," Laura said. "I want to see it. I may have to give it some thought before I decide, but I want to see it all."

They went into the hallway and through several other rooms, up an interior staircase, and emerged just outside the room with the three windows and the balcony. It had been part of a large apartment that hadn't been lived in for years. But despite the broken window, it was in better condition than the lower floor, and Laura knew beyond a doubt that it was what she wanted.

Her next step was to find someone to help her redesign the interior, and by next spring she would be open. Concealing her rekindled joy, she turned to Mrs. Sanderson. "I may want to bring someone else in to look at it. The location is ideal. And if it's structurally possible to make the changes I would need to make, we may have a deal."

Mrs. Sanderson smiled and visibly relaxed. "Just call me. You can pick up the key and come by yourself if you'd like."

With mutual thanks they departed the building, and Laura practically floated across the cobblestones and up the steep staircase cut into the rock wall. Over the years the edges of the stone steps had been hollowed and smoothed by centuries of footsteps. Echoes of history swirled around her until she could almost hear the ring of boot heels and the clang of swords against the stone or the soft swish of crinolines and satin slippers as ladies of years long past hurried away from the river.

Laura closed her eyes and took a deep breath. Soon she would be a part of that history. Soon she and the ancient river would live and work side by side.

Chapter Three

As Laura headed out of Savannah, her elation began to diminish, and the reality of the challenge ahead weighed on her once again. It wasn't as if she didn't know what she was doing. After all, this wasn't the first business she had started.

With a thoughtful frown she leaned forward, turned down the radio and adjusted the speed of her windshield wipers. Autumn leaves in early shades of yellow and orange clung to the edges of the wet pavement and littered the wooded countryside. A hard rain drove onto the windshield of her car.

Snug in the cocoon of her bucket seat, she couldn't help wondering if maybe the problem was that she did know what she was doing. Maybe she realized all too well that getting the tearoom in Savannah off the ground would take all the money she had and still leave her hip-deep in debt.

But when she had stood in the middle of that barren, dirty room and stared through those tall, grime-encrusted windows at the river below, she'd felt a sense of homecoming, of rightness, and it was the first truly good feeling she'd had in months.

Out of habit she glanced at the speedometer, then grimaced and lightened her pressure on the accelerator. The combination of tension and daydreams always seemed to give her a lead foot, and lately she seemed to spend a lot of her time backing off the accelerator.

Deliberately slowing even more, she watched the rain as it filtered through the forest's canopy to drip softly onto the fallen leaves at the side of the road. It was a peaceful sight, but at the same time somehow lonely.

She turned the radio up again and brought her attention to the road ahead. Inside the canyon of overhanging trees the waning day had faded to dark already, an early and sudden darkness that had come with the rain. In the gloom and the pounding rain Laura felt especially alone on the two-lane highway that led south out of Savannah. There was nothing much out that way but farm land, a few scattered small towns and her father's horse farm.

An old, bluesy love song came on the radio, and without warning, as clearly as if he stood before her, she could see Houston. The thought of him wrapped itself around her with the kind of ease that told her he had never been far away.

Houston. She rolled the name silently over her tongue, enjoying the feel of it. So far he had been nothing but pleasant surprises and kindness, but he was a problem just the same, one more complication in a life that was already overloaded with them.

Goodness knows, it wasn't that she didn't like him, because she did, no matter how hard she tried not to. Every instinct in her screamed that the timing was all wrong, but still she couldn't get him out of her mind.

In the middle of a thought, there he'd be. With his laughing blue eyes and his plaid shirt and tight, faded jeans. And those boots. Those awful, ugly boots.

For the life of her she couldn't figure out how someone who looked so unprosperous could afford to play polo. It wasn't exactly an inexpensive sport. But maybe that was where all his money went. She smiled, then chuckled at the thought. At this point, any little flaw in the man was more than welcome.

Oh, and there *were* flaws. Anyone who went from football to bull riding to polo lived a life that was hovering between reckless and suicidal. And if the number of tiny scars she'd already noticed were any indication, he was well beyond simply reckless.

Tempting as he was, she wasn't that big a fool. Laura eased up on the accelerator again and looked around her. The forest had thinned, and in its place were pecan groves. Tranquil giant trees spread their limbs tall and wide across deeply shadowed lawns.

Pale light glowed weakly from the dark gray sky. Thunder rumbled in the distance, and the rain slackened, intensified and slackened again in the few minutes it took for the pecan grove on her right to give way to the white pipe fencing of Warner land.

Laura slowed and turned onto a gravel road strad-
dled by a wrought-iron arch that spelled out The Polo
Station in foot-high block letters.

When she had first returned after years of absence,
it had been a shock to see how much the farm had
changed since she had left it as a child. Then, the rich
plantation land that had been in the Warner family
since the 1700s had been farmland. Now a few share-
croppers still lived on the outlying acres, but the land's
heart had shifted from raising crops to training polo
ponies and players.

On sunny days the open pastures were filled with the
sturdy, spirited horses who were the soul of the light-
ning-paced game. Today the empty acres looked sad
under their misty veil of rain, as if they, too, felt a little lost.

Laura pulled her eyes from the gray emptiness beside her and focused on the road that led straight
ahead through acre after flat acre. The land's surface
was dotted here and there with small stands of trees,
with nothing else to break the monotony but inter-
secting pipe fencing.

Over time she had gradually grown used to the
changes that had taken place in her home, but she still
occasionally felt like a stranger on land that held some
of her fondest memories.

The important thing, she reminded herself often,
was that her father was happy with the life he had
created for himself. He had a reason for living again,
and that was something his family, as hard as they had
tried, hadn't been able to give him.

It was for his happiness that Laura tried to be glad,
but it wasn't always easy. And the passing of time only

seemed to make it that much harder. She had been too sure that they could learn to be father and daughter again. To watch Max pull farther away from her with each day that went by hurt unbearably.

She was glad he was well again. But while he had needed her, while he was so sick and wanted her near him, she had dared to dream that the two of them could make up for all the years they had been apart.

For as long as she lived, she would never forget the fear that had overwhelmed her after Etta's call. On the nonstop drive from Arkansas, when she thought Max would die before she could reach him, her grief had been almost unbearable.

And in the two months he had lingered near death, it was as if the intervening fourteen years had dropped away. She had sat with him, held his hand, read to him. She had refused to leave his side, fighting for his life the same way she had as a child, willing him to live with her every thought and breath.

And again, just as she had with the first battle, she had won and she had lost. For the second time she had watched him grow stronger and more distant with each day. She wouldn't have believed it could hurt more the second time, but it had.

When she was twelve, she hadn't understood why he had pushed his family away, and she didn't understand it any more today than she had fourteen years ago. She only knew that whatever demons had driven him then were with him still. They might be weaker, but they still had the power to devastate her, and she wouldn't wait around to be torn apart the same way twice.

She couldn't turn her back and just walk away as her mother had. But she couldn't live in the same house with him, either. She had to create a separate place for herself. Maybe someday she could find a bridge across the chasm that separated them, but not today.

The road ahead was a solid blur as Laura switched the windshield wipers to full speed. She sniffed unconsciously while the blur grew steadily worse. She blinked hard in sudden alarm, trying to focus, and when she rubbed her eyes, the back of her hand came away wet.

Blindly her fingertips searched her face and found cheeks streaked with tears she hadn't known she was shedding. The mad pounding of the windshield wipers fought with the radio to drown out her ragged sobs as she worked to clear her eyes, yet the tears only flowed faster.

With one hand she clung to a steering wheel that jerked fiercely against her efforts, while with the back of the other hand she wiped at the flow of tears until finally her vision cleared to a dim haze.

And through the haze she saw not the road but a wall of solid black. Too startled to scream, Laura slammed on the brakes and looked desperately for a way out, but the car had only begun to slow when its front end canted sharply downward and its rear slid sideways through the mud and gravel that edged the road. With a hard jolt the car came to a sudden stop that jarred Laura's teeth as her shoulder harness locked and halted her forward momentum.

Stunned, she searched frantically for an explanation of the roadblock that had put her into a skid. But she summoned only the dim memory of a tall stand of trees where the road took a sharp turn. She knew the road straightened out again, and the paddock area was only a short distance farther.

The car was nose down in a ditch on the wrong side of the road, and the house was a long way off for someone in her one good silk suit and her best high heels.

With a frustrated moan, Laura unbuckled her seat belt, folded her arms across the top of the steering wheel and leaned her forehead against her arms. She was too mad at herself to be sad or even frightened.

She loved her car. She'd sold everything else she'd owned, and it was one of the few things left in the world that was truly her own. She loved it, and because of her stupid daydreaming she had just wrecked it. Her eyes burned fiercely with the return of tears she was determined not to shed.

Over the blaring of the radio and the thudding of the windshield wipers, she almost didn't hear the sudden, sharp rap of knuckles on the passenger window. While she debated whether or not to check her makeup before she rolled down the window, the rapping became more insistent and then suddenly stopped altogether.

She shrugged and didn't even lift her head from the steering wheel. She was almost glad whoever it was had gone. She was still too upset to talk to anyone, and she must look like pure hell.

Then, without warning, two hard, rapid blows shattered the passenger window and rained glass pebbles across the interior of the car. Laura let out a single shocked, angry shriek as a man's hand reached in, unlocked the door and pulled it open.

"Where are you hurt?" Houston slid into the seat next to her without bothering to brush away the bits of safety glass.

Outrage had overtaken her so completely that Laura forgot about her smeared makeup and that she had just driven her car into a ditch. "You broke my window!" she shouted indignantly.

Houston's brows knitted with concern. He leaned closer, turned off the radio and spoke carefully. "Are you hurt?"

"No!" she snapped.

He brushed her cheek with his fingertips. "You've been crying."

Remembering her makeup, Laura drew back from him. "Go away."

He smiled gently. "But I came to rescue you."

"I'm fine," she said, wanting desperately to hide her face behind her hands.

Houston turned off the windshield wipers. "No offense, but I find that hard to believe."

Laura turned her head and stared straight ahead at the dark, rain-distorted world beyond her windshield. The pine-woods scent of his after-shave warmed her in spite of the wet, chill air that filled the car.

There was a time in every woman's life when she longed for the kind of feelings that Houston had evoked in Laura from the moment she had first looked into his eyes—feelings that would become memories she could carry with her through the years to come, memories she could hold close when the nights were cold and empty.

But this was not one of those times, at least not in Laura's life. This was a time when she had too many conflicting emotions and too many memories to deal with already. There was no room in her life for a man like Houston. But she did need to get home.

"Could you pull me out?" she asked in a very small voice.

"Why don't we just see if I can back the car out first?"

She turned her head until they were almost face to face and let her eyes traverse the remaining distance. "What do you want me to do?"

"Slide over here, and I'll come around." He got out, brushed off the car seat and held out his hand to help her.

Laura looked at him, looked at his hand and looked at the floor console she had to get past. With a sigh of resignation, she took his hand. "This isn't going to be easy." She drew her knees up between the steering wheel and the console. Her straight skirt hugged her thighs, and despite the little six-inch slit in the back, it was impossible for her to move her legs as anything but a unit.

As she debated the best way to get her calves over the floor shift, Houston smiled sweetly and asked, "Anything I can do?"

"You could close your eyes." She tucked her knees in closer to her chest and slid the soles of her shoes along the dashboard while her legs skimmed over the top of the gear shift.

Houston watched closely while her skirt rode up to the middle of her thighs and her shapely calves slid across the top of the console and down into the vacant passenger seat. "Suggest something realistic," he answered.

Laura caught the hem of her skirt with her free hand and tugged futilely toward her knees. Nothing budged, including her rear end, which remained solidly in the driver's seat. "I think maybe I do need some help here." She stared into his sapphire eyes and couldn't help laughing. "I'm stuck."

Houston smiled at her. "I kind of hate to do anything about it. You look very fetching like that, Miss Warner."

"I don't feel fetching." She tugged at the hand he still held, encouraging him to do something besides look at her. "I feel silly."

He leaned into the car, braced his knee on the edge of the seat and put her hand on his shoulder. "I guess there's no easy way to get over a floor console while you're wearing a tight skirt."

His face was inches from hers, and Laura felt suddenly breathless. "I guess there isn't," she agreed. "Especially with the car leaning the other way."

"You're going to have to hold your arms up a little so I can get my hands under them. I'll have to lift you."

Her stomach turned over with a thud as she realized how intimate the situation had become. She obediently lifted her arms, then put her hand on the back of his neck and tried not to notice how it made her feel.

"Isn't this going to be a little hard on your back?"
she asked weakly.

Sliding his hands under her arms, he smiled again
as he felt her grip tighten. "I've wrestled steers a lot
heavier than you are, Laura, hon." He lifted her
against his chest. Her hair brushed his cheek as he
talked. "I don't think this is anything for you to worry
about."

Hon, she thought. Short for honey. A term of en-
dearment Laura had always regarded as particularly
nauseating. So why had her heart just fluttered ever so
delicately? And why did his arms feel so good around
her as he gently lifted her against him and guided her
into the passenger seat?

With her body tucked snugly under his and the top
of her head brushing the underside of his chin, Houston drew his head back and stared into her eyes. So
close that if she breathed too deeply her lips would be
touching his, he held her there for one long, heart-
stopping moment before he pulled his hands from
under her arms and straightened. Then without another word he went around the car and sat behind the
steering wheel.

The car started with no problem, and for a minute
it rocked back with a promising lurch. Then the tires
began to spin, and the rear of the car slid sideways and
a few inches deeper into the ditch.

While Houston tried again, Laura tried to forget
that instant when the world had seemed to stop and
she had been certain he was going to kiss her. She
stared out the broken window and searched the area
outside for his car as her pulse rate gradually returned
to normal.

Outside she saw nothing but a dark, wet night and an empty road. She was about to question him when he turned off the motor and handed her the keys.

"We'll pull it out tomorrow. You stay here while I get a slicker for you."

"Where are you parked?"

He answered very slowly while his eyes inspected her all the way down to her shoes. "I guess you could say I'm parked under a tree behind you." His gaze traveled slowly up, and his expression flickered between appreciation and apprehension. "You certainly do look nice." His eyes reached hers and stayed there while a soft look of affectionate amusement filled them. "I'm riding a horse."

Without looking down, Laura visualized her lined silk skirt, her sheer stockings, the slender heels of her soft leather pumps. All these things were designed to come no closer to a horse than the opposite side of a paddock fence. "No way," she said levelly.

He shook his head. "No problem. The slicker'll keep you dry. You ride sidesaddle in front of me. I'll hold you on."

"Western saddle?"

"Yeah."

"Are you planning to balance me on top of the saddle horn?" she asked with a trace of sarcasm she simply couldn't help. Visions of the console fiasco still danced in her head.

"No." He smiled. "I'm planning to balance you in my lap. Very cozy."

Laura felt a sudden rush at the image his words conjured. Very cozy, indeed. "I get my own slicker?" she asked without much enthusiasm.

"All yours." He held out a wet arm. "I wasn't wearing one."

With a sigh, she gave in. It beat walking, and she'd get home a lot faster than if she waited for someone to bring a car for her. Overlooking her powerful and unwanted physical awareness of him for the moment, she was lucky Houston had been there, and it was probably about time she told him so.

"Thank you," she said in the same small voice she had used earlier. "It would have been a pretty miserable evening if you hadn't come along."

Houston laughed. "Instead of the evening of fun and comfort that it has been."

"Well," Laura said with a smile and a shrug, "it could have been worse."

"Yeah," he said, suddenly very serious. "I wasn't going to bring this up, but what the hell were you doing? When I saw you coming down that road, I just knew you were going right through those trees. It looked like you were planning to commit suicide and then chickened out."

It wasn't funny, and Laura tried to hide the unseemly giggle that bubbled up inside her. "Is that why you broke out the window?"

Still plainly agitated, he said, "Your head was resting on the steering wheel, and you weren't moving."

Laura sobered, realizing she had really scared him. "It's a long story." She didn't want to think about why he would care so much.

Houston touched her cheek with his fingertip, sorry for his outburst. "Why don't I get you home first? After that, I've got all night." His rich, deep voice sounded tender as he drew his finger along the curve of her chin. "And I like long stories."

Without waiting for an answer, he opened the car door and stepped into the wet night. While Laura waited for his return, she locked her purse in the glove compartment and composed herself. The ride was going to be bad enough without having to hold a clutch bag. She slipped her keys into the pocket of her suit jacket.

Just as she was beginning to wonder again if this was such a bright idea, the door next to her opened and Houston reached inside to take her hand. "Be careful. It's muddy right here." He helped her out and all but carried her the few feet to the road.

She shivered as he held the slicker for her. The rain was a steady, fine mist, and the temperature had dropped to a prewinter chill. She gratefully burrowed into the oversize slicker. While Houston pulled it closed around her neck and buttoned the top buttons, Laura searched for her fingertips inside the sleeves.

"I feel like a kid inside a big brother's snowsuit." She held her arms out in front of her, no fingers in sight. "Help me. I can't find my hands."

He left the task of buttoning her up and began to roll back the left sleeve until her fingertips emerged. "How far?" he asked.

"One more turn." She watched him bent over the task of dressing her. Beads of water clung to his hair; his shirt was thoroughly wet; and yet all his attention was on her comfort. "Aren't you cold?" she asked softly, and touched a darkly glistening curl that had fallen across his forehead.

In spite of the cold and the rain and the wreck, she suddenly, unwillingly, felt warm and fluttery inside.

He stepped back, shook his head and smiled. "I grew up on a ranch, so this is nothing." His eyes followed the yellow slicker down to her ankles, and his smile became a chuckle. "You're not real tall, are you?"

Laura frowned and continued buttoning the slicker where he had left off. "This thing's probably big on you, too."

He knelt and began fastening it from the hem up. "Not this big. You're beginning to look like a kid again."

"A what?" she asked sharply. "And what do you mean *again*?"

Houston cleared his throat. "Never mind."

Before she could press further, he scooped her up in his arms and began to carry her toward his horse. "I think I'd better get you home now."

Laura's voice rose to a startled squeak. "I *can* walk, you know."

He looked into her huge eyes just inches from his. "Those shoes are too nice to ruin tromping through the countryside."

"But I feel—" her words faded to a whisper "—funny." Then her voice came back stronger. "And if you tell me you've carried calves heavier than me, I swear I'll scream."

Houston laughed. "Well, I guess that leaves me pretty speechless, then." He slowed and picked his way down the banks of the ditch and up the other side to the edge of the trees where his horse was tethered. He stopped beside a stump. "I'm going to put you here.

It'll keep you out of the weeds, and it's high enough that I can lift you onto the horse without any trouble.''

He stood Laura on the uneven top of the stump. Again they were eye to eye, and the cold night suddenly felt kissed with the heat of summer. His hands remained on her waist while she steadied herself. Even through the slicker, she was conscious of his touch, and more than conscious of the scant inches that separated them. His lips were so close she could feel the warm whisper of his breath. Frozen between anticipation and apprehension, Laura closed her eyes and drew in a deep, shuddering breath.

When his hands left her waist, she felt abandoned, and when she opened her eyes again, he was walking away. She watched him swing effortlessly onto the back of his horse and guide it to the edge of the stump.

As she stared at him, she couldn't help wondering how this night would end and if she would ever have another one like it. Strangely, when she thought of how close she was to being safe and warm in her own bed, it was with a sense of sadness.

"Turn around," Houston said, twirling his finger in a circle. "I need to lift you from behind."

Without comment, Laura turned and stood still, waiting for his next instruction. Not since childhood had she blindly trusted anyone the way she found herself trusting Houston.

When her father had been injured, she'd helped her mother nurse him through that first harrowing year, right up until they had left him. Then, two years after they had moved in with her mother's family in Arkansas, Laura's grandfather had suffered a stroke, and she had helped her mother and grandmother with round-the-clock nursing. Being on the receiving end of the kind of nurturing attention that Houston gave so easily was something she wasn't used to, but it was something she knew she could learn to enjoy.

Houston's arm, when it slid around her waist, caught her by surprise. Slowly, he guided her back a step as he eased the horse closer. Laura clasped his forearm with both hands as his arm tightened around her and he began to lift.

"Steady," he whispered just above her ear. "Let me do the work."

She felt her hip press against the tensed muscles of his leg and slide across his thigh as he lifted her higher.

"Lean back against my chest," he instructed softly. "And wrap your arm around my neck."

Laura did as she was told and found herself squarely in his lap. They were arm in arm and face to face. She blinked and swallowed hard. "Is this it?"

His mouth twitched, but he didn't smile. "One more thing." His hand cupped her thighs and lifted her higher on the cradle of his legs. When he slid his hand away, the pressure of the saddle horn against her hip was negligible. "How's that?"

"Wonderful." She couldn't help smiling. Then another thought replaced the smile with a light frown. "You're awfully good at this."

"I used to ride my brother's kids like this until they were big enough to ride alone."

"Uh-huh." She mulled his answer over suspiciously. "Well, you certainly have it down to a science."

His chin nuzzled her hair. "Does that mean you're comfortable?"

She was very conscious of the muscled breadth of his shoulder against her palm. Her fingers curved over the hard surface and, instead of cold dampness, she felt warmth radiate into her palm. How, she wondered, could anything feel so good on such a miserable night?

"Well, I probably won't have to worry about falling asleep up here," she said, and wished she felt as unaffected as she was trying to sound.

He kicked the horse into a gentle walk, staying close to the trees. Even at a slow pace, their bodies swayed together in an uneven rhythm, rocking against each other first one way and then the other, but always touching.

As they neared the first paddock, he pulled her even closer to him. When he nosed the horse into the ditch, Houston's body pitched sharply forward, shoving Laura hard against the saddle horn.

"Oops," he whispered in her ear. "Sorry."

They started up the other side, and their bodies shifted in the opposite direction. Helpless against gravity, Laura slid backward, even more tightly than before, into the wide V of Houston's legs and the open cradle at the juncture of his thighs.

She gasped as he groaned, and she tried to wiggle away until Houston caught her tightly around the waist.

"Hold still," he said in a voice that was more plea than command.

"Sorry," Laura whispered, wishing she could die.

After a minute he let his breath out with a sigh and said, "Not that it wasn't nice."

Back on level ground, Laura tried not to let her mind wander to the lap she was sitting in and the arms that were holding her there, but it wasn't easy. When she felt something warm and soft brush her temple, a part of her hoped it was only his chin.

They passed the first series of paddocks in silence. At the stable, a weak light glowed over the empty parking area. Laura lifted her head and searched, determined to find a car where there was none.

"Where is everybody?" she asked weakly.

Houston cleared his throat and made no move to loosen his hold on her. "It's kind of late."

"Where's your car?" Laura knew better than to wiggle loose, but it wasn't easy to hold still. The ride had begun to feel much too good, and she urgently wanted to get off that horse.

Houston tightened the outside rein to keep the horse heading straight. "I walked down to the stables."

She planted a hand in the middle of his chest and pushed herself away until she could look him in the eye. "In the rain?"

He shrugged. "If you're planning to go riding in the rain, you might as well walk in the rain."

"What do we do now?" Laura felt as if all hope was gone, and she didn't care if she sounded like it. She hadn't realized how tired she was.

Houston almost laughed, but he held it in. Then he pressed her head onto his wet shoulder and guided the horse past the stable it kept trying to turn toward. "I'll take you on to the house, then I'll bring the horse back."

"That won't work," she complained against the soft haven of his neck. "Then I'll be warm and dry and you'll still be out in the cold rain."

He patted her shoulder consolingly. "I'll be all right. The horse'll find his own way back, and I can follow him in my car."

Laura was so relieved she felt like crying again. For a minute she'd been afraid she was never going to get in out of the rain, because she couldn't have let Houston walk home after all he'd done for her, yet there was no one but her to go with him to the stables.

"Relieved?" he asked.

"Immensely," she said, not bothering with a polite lie.

He laughed softly, and after they had left the light of the stables behind, he said just above a whisper, "You know, Miss Warner, I like you a lot."

The heart palpitations that she had fought all evening returned with dizzying speed. She enjoyed and despised her thoughts at the same time. When he had first met her, she had not been dressed to make a great impression. And this evening she had gone through progressively worsening stages of dishevelment to reach what must be the all-time low point in her physical appearance. On top of that, she must seem like a walking accident. *Why* would he like her?

"Thank you," she said quietly after a long pause.

"Thank you? That's it? No reciprocating sentiment? Not even an 'I like you, too, Mr. Carder'?"

She lifted her head and stared at him. "Well, of course, I like you. You've been terribly kind. More than kind, considering the way I reacted when you punched in my window. And I'm extremely grate—"

"If this is your 'I'm beholden to you, stranger' speech, you can keep it," he interrupted. Houston pulled the horse to a smooth halt and looked into her face. "That wasn't what I meant. And you know it."

Flustered by the flame in Houston's eyes and the thud of her own heart, Laura instinctively drew away. And it might have worked if she hadn't been sitting in his lap on top of a horse.

As it was, she tipped too far back, her legs flew up, and Houston had to grab her with both arms to keep her from falling. It was when he pulled her against him that her weight shifted to that area of his anatomy she had worked so futilely all evening to avoid.

From the soft moan that rattled from Houston's throat, it was obvious that he had noticed it as well. With no wasted motion, his mouth closed over hers in a kiss that left no doubt as to the depth of his sudden desire.

Heat seared through Laura in a wave that swept to her toes, and the rush of emotion that followed was sweet. She clung to him with an abandon that would have shocked her had she stopped to think about it. But she didn't. She was lost in the feel of his velvet kiss, lost in the forest scent of him.

With a contented growl, Houston wrapped her still tighter in his arms and snuggled his body more solidly under her. And for a moment longer, Laura lingered in the warm, heady world of his embrace.

Then, like a chilling blast, logic returned and she stiffened and broke the kiss. Embarrassed and confused by her reactions, she hid her face against his neck and waited for him to release her.

For the second time that evening she felt something warm and soft brush against her hair, and this time she knew it was not his chin.

"I'm sorry, sweetheart," Houston said quietly. "I guess I surprised you a little, huh?"

He gathered in the reins with one hand while holding her to him with the other, and once again he nudged the horse into motion. "Laura," he said after a small silence, "you're not very experienced, are you?"

She straightened from her defensive tuck and stared at him incredulously. "I'm not very *what*?"

He smiled. "That's not an insult, sweetheart. It's just that I keep getting this feeling of...innocence from you."

"Don't you think that's a little personal?"

"Well, I'm having some pretty personal feelings about you right now."

"Houston," she said with a ragged sigh, "I've had better days."

"You don't want to talk about it right now?"

"Not particularly."

"Would you like to know about me?"

"No."

"Well, I'm not exactly what you'd consider innocent," he said, telling her anyway. "But compared to my brothers, I've practically been a choirboy."

Interested in spite of herself, Laura started to ask him about his brothers, then stopped herself. The more she knew about him, the more risk she ran of caring. His family didn't matter. In a few days his visit with her father would be finished, and Houston would return to wherever he had come from. And she would go on with her life.

In the spring her tearoom would be open, and if he returned to the Polo Station, she might never know it. She had spent enough of her life sitting in sickrooms, silently piecing together jigsaw puzzles while she listened for someone she loved to take his next breath and prayed that it wouldn't be his last.

She shuddered at the thought, and Houston tightened his arm around her.

"Just a little farther," he said softly. He pointed ahead with his rein hand. "You can see the house now."

Laura turned her head, and indeed the house was a dark outline against the gloom of the sky. It was a huge house, built in the twenties, when money had been plentiful and ostentation had been a way of life. But the cost of maintaining the old mansion was enormous, and finally Max had been forced to turn the unprofitable farm into a polo clinic and breeding farm to keep the estate intact.

"What time is it?" she asked, searching the unlit facade for a sign of life.

Houston checked his watch. "Almost nine. I guess Max has turned in already."

"His room's at the back of the house, anyway. So is Etta's."

"Are you hungry?"

"More exhausted than anything." She couldn't help sighing as she thought of the soft, warm bed waiting for her. Any sadness that she might have felt earlier was long gone. All she wanted now was a hot bath and a flannel nightgown.

"I didn't offend you, did I?"

"What?"

"When I kissed you. The way you pulled away, I thought maybe I had."

"No. No, I wasn't offended. It was just, well, I didn't want it to get too serious." She shrugged, trying to seem more relaxed than she felt. "After all, it was a product of the moment. Nothing more."

"A product of the moment, huh?" Houston repeated coolly.

"Well, that's all it was. If I hadn't been sitting in your lap, on the back of a horse, in the middle of nowhere, it would never have happened."

"Maybe it wouldn't have happened tonight. But if I had anything to say about it, it *would* have happened."

Her stomach flip-flopped, and she could have kicked herself for it. He was a stranger who was passing through her life. That's all he was, and he would never be anything more. "We hardly know each other," she said stiffly, to herself as much as to him.

"We've got time."

"I doubt that there will be enough."

"Why? Is it because I play polo?"

"That's one good reason. And I'm sure I could think of others." At least she was sure she was going to try.

"Why did your mother leave?"

The gentle question came out of left field, and all Laura's fight was expelled in a huff that turned into a sigh. "That's another long story," she said wearily.

Houston guided the horse around the flower beds in the front lawn and pulled up next to the raised terrace that fronted the house. "You still owe me the first story."

Laura looked wistfully at the house, then at him. "Another night? I'm afraid by the time I get dried off and into some warm clothes, I'm going to be falling asleep."

He nodded and, without a word, lowered her onto the terrace. "I'll be around." He gave her a casual parting salute and rode off toward the garage.

Laura stood for a moment in the rain, watching him, then she turned and went into the house.

Chapter Four

Laura strolled out of the steamy bathroom wrapped in a pale lavender bath sheet. With one corner of it she slowly dried her dark blond hair while adroitly avoiding her reflection in the cheval glass on the other side of the bedroom. Left to dry on its own, her hair took on the look of an electrified halo.

It wasn't exactly the most flattering hairstyle. But on a quiet night like this one, with the rain pattering gently against the house, there was no one around to impress. So Laura continued to avoid looking at herself in the mirror and wandered across the room to hang the damp towel over the bathroom door.

Then she went to her bureau, opened a sachet-scented drawer and took out a matching set of tap pants and camisole top in petal-pink silk. She slid on the tap pants, closed the bureau drawer and reached for a box of dusting powder. Suddenly her hand went instead to her stomach, which had begun to give off sudden, insistent signals of ravenous hunger.

She hurriedly covered herself with a flurry of dusting powder, then pulled on the camisole, stepped into the big, fuzzy bedroom slippers at the foot of her bed and cinched the waist of her ankle-length chenille robe. Then she went down the stairs toward the kitchen.

She pushed open the swinging door between dining room and kitchen, flipped on the light and sniffed at the faint odor of chocolate in the air. Rainy nights and steaming mugs of cocoa, topped with melting marshmallows, would be forever linked in Laura's childhood memories.

The soles of her slippers scuffed softly on the colorful ceramic tile floor as she crossed to the refrigerator, took out eggs, milk and cheese, then went to the island in the middle of the room where a pan of cocoa sat warming on a burner turned low. It was only then that Laura took her first look around the room and discovered Houston watching her from the breakfast nook on the far side of the kitchen.

It was too late to run, so she nodded hesitantly and said, "Uh, hello."

He smiled and saluted her with his mug. "I'm having hot chocolate. What are you having?"

"An omelet." She held up an egg.

He hooked a thumb in the direction of the stove top. "There's plenty of cocoa left, if you want some."

"Thanks." She smiled fleetingly. "I can make this for two, if you want."

Houston's grin widened. "Sounds good. Can I help?"

"No need." Laura turned to the stove and resisted the urge to run a hand through her hair. She had already walked the entire length of the room with no makeup, hair out of a horror movie and in those damned fuzzy slippers.

There was nothing she could do now to retrieve the situation, but she couldn't help wondering what he was doing there. "I thought you would be staying at the guest lodge," she said over her shoulder, trying not to make it sound as if she wished he were somewhere else, which all but a small part of her did.

"No, I always stay up here," he answered casually. "I thought Etta told you that."

Stifling a groan, she wondered where her mind had gone. She knew where he was staying. "Oh, yeah," she said lamely, "I don't know what I was thinking of."

Laura fussed with the bowls and pan, wistfully entertaining the thought of walking out of the room. So far she had managed to look like the bride of Frankenstein and sound like the village idiot, and she had either fallen off or run into something every time she got near him. After a time she carefully folded the omelet over and flipped it.

She then sliced the omelet in two with the spatula and laid each piece on a separate plate. With great care she balanced her plate on top of her mug, picked up his plate with her free hand and carried both meals to the table.

"Wouldn't a tray have been easier?" Houston couldn't help asking as he stood to rescue her plate from its precarious perch. He leaned across the table and set it down.

Irritated, Laura caught herself just before she slammed her mug onto the tabletop. "Houston…" she said through gritted teeth.

"I know," he answered, sitting again. "You've had better days, and you're not in the mood."

"Thank you." She sat across from him and stared at her plate. The ravenous hunger that had brought her downstairs was gone.

"This omelet's great."

"Thank you." She picked up her mug and stared at the melting marshmallows. She felt like a robot, a barely polite and very uncomfortable robot. If he had only had the light on, she would never have come into the kitchen. And what had he been doing sitting alone in the dark anyway?

Looking up, she asked the question aloud.

"Me?" Houston asked while his face went from dumbfounded to carefully blank and finally to sheepish.

Laura almost laughed. She had never seen him at a loss, and she really enjoyed not being the only one who was uncomfortable. She took a drink of cocoa and felt her appetite coming back. "You," she said when he looked as if he had found his tongue again.

Houston stared at the tabletop and rearranged the salt and pepper shakers several times before he finally said, "You see, I come from a family of five kids. And I used to go out to the back porch at night, just to be alone." His gaze slowly left the shakers and found its way to Laura's face. "I'd sit out there in the dark, where it was quiet, and watch the stars and listen to the night sounds.''

His look wasn't sheepish anymore. It was soft as moonlight, and his voice caressed each word. ''And after a while somebody would always join me, and we'd sit and talk, just watching the stars and listening to the night.''

Laura felt the bite of omelet she'd just swallowed turn to dust in her dry throat. She should have run when she wanted to. ''I didn't come down here looking for you,'' she said, almost choking.

Houston gently shoved her mug closer to her and shrugged. ''Maybe I was just wishing you would.'' He paused and looked a little wistful. ''We can still talk, can't we? There's so much I don't know about you. And you do owe me those stories.''

Laura took another bite of omelet and tried to ignore him long enough to repair her ragged emotions. But her efforts were largely in vain.

The source of her misery had come in from the rain and changed into fresh jeans and a pullover sweater with a deep V neck. There was no shirt underneath to block her view of the exposed wedge of Houston's smoothly tanned chest or to blunt the outline of well-formed muscles under the thin cotton knit of the sweater.

Taking another bite and hoping that she wouldn't choke, Laura forced her eyes away from the exposed wedge of his bare chest and all that it hinted at and moved on. His hair was still wet. Combed straight back like a sleek, dark cap, it framed his face and pulled at her gaze like a magnet.

Finally Houston quit waiting for her to answer him and went back to eating. With his attention on other things, Laura contemplated his high, broad forehead, hooded, intense eyes and strong, straight nose that was a little too bold for perfection. Just above his taut, sculptured jawline was the one feature that was absolutely mesmerizing—a full, sensuous mouth that must have been made just for kissing. . . .

"I thought your hair was straight," he said suddenly.

"What?" With a jerk, Laura fumbled toward reality from the depths of her contemplation. As she fought the urge, once again, to comb her fingers through her hair, she wondered nervously if he had seen her studying him, or if he, heaven forbid, had been too caught up in scrutinizing her to notice.

"Your hair. I thought it was straight."

"Whatever made you think that?" she asked with just a trace of breathlessness.

"Well, it just looked so different earlier."

"Blow dryers and hot rollers can work miracles." She took a deep breath and felt her heartbeat begin to slow.

"Actually, it doesn't look too bad like that." He turned his head and narrowed his eyes as if that would somehow affect the view. "A little wild, maybe, but interesting."

For want of a better reply, Laura laughed weakly and shrugged. "I wasn't expecting to see anybody at this time of night," she confessed, thinking as much of her furry hot-pink slippers as she was of her hair.

"Ah," Houston said, nodding. Then, with an impish grin, he asked, "What, if anything, are you wearing between those fuzzy shoes and that belt that does such a lousy job of holding your robe together?''

Laura opened her mouth, but words refused to form. She cleared her throat and tried again. "Uh, pajamas. Sort of.''

He nodded again. "Ones with no legs, I guess.''

"They do exist.''

"Baby dolls?'' he offered.

"Tap pants,'' Laura said stiffly.

Houston brightened. "Oh, I like those. But I thought they were underwear.''

Laura handed him her cup. "Why don't you go fix us some more hot chocolate while we think of something else to talk about?''

Still grinning, he took their mugs and headed toward the island stove top.

"And I like lots of marshmallows,'' she called after him.

While he poured the milk and stirred in the cocoa, he said over his shoulder, "Did I leave out the part about how attractive your legs are?''

"Another subject,'' Laura said firmly.

"Okay, then, how about story number two? Why did your mother leave?''

"If this is what you did to your brothers out on that back porch, I'm amazed any of them ever came for a second chat.''

"And sisters,'' Houston corrected. "Two brothers. Two sisters. But you're trying to change the subject, and I'm far too clever to let you get away with it.''

"I hate this,'' she grumbled.

"Do it anyway. It's good for you. And I'm curious.''

Laura sighed and began slowly. She couldn't remember ever talking about the time after her father's accident, and the words she chose to start with were as much a surprise to her as they were to Houston. "I never understood. I never understood the way he acted. And I never understood how she could leave."

"I know this can't be easy, Laura." Houston turned to face her, leaning his hips against the counter. "I already know that Max pretty much drove you away. And I know that even though his actions were aimed mainly at your mother, a lot of his bitterness must have fallen on you and your sister, too."

Laura nodded and pulled the robe tighter around her while tension knotted her muscles and sent a shiver down her spine. "At first it wasn't so bad," she said, taking a deep, steadying breath. "None of us believed he wasn't going to get better, not even him. Mom and I sat with him almost constantly. At first I read to pass the time, but I'd get restless, so then I started working on jigsaw puzzles instead."

She wished Houston would hurry with the cocoa. She was so cold her teeth were starting to chatter. "After a couple of months," she said, rubbing her arms to warm herself, "Dad was well enough to sit up, and he and I used to work at the puzzles together. It was after he got the wheelchair that everything changed." Her voice dropped to a gravelly whisper. "Maybe it was then he realized he was never going to get any better."

Houston cleared his throat quietly and asked in as gentle a tone as he could manage, "How long was it before your mother took you and left?"

"A little over a year. I used to blame her for everything. I hadn't wanted to go, and it wasn't until I came back that I realized what that year must have been like for Mom."

Houston set both mugs of cocoa on the table and stood for a minute, looking at Laura. Then he caught both her hands and held them cupped between his palms. "Your fingers are like ice. It makes you nervous to talk about this, doesn't it?"

He wrapped her hands around one mug of steaming cocoa, then moved behind her chair. "Did I put in enough marshmallows?" he asked softly while he gripped her shoulders and squeezed gently. His thumbs moved to the tightly bunched muscles on either side of her spine and pressed in and upward through the soft fabric of her robe.

A delicious, relaxing shiver ran up her back, and Laura sighed. Without thinking, she let her head roll to the side and felt the back of Houston's hand brush her cheek. His fingers slid over her shoulder and splayed across her collarbone while his thumbs stroked up her neck in a smooth, firm glide.

"Oh, my goodness," Laura groaned. "Don't tell me, on top of everything else, you give massages, too."

"I'm just an all-around handyman," he answered in a voice both deep and tender.

His hands played over her neck and shoulders with firm caresses until she felt as soft and pliable as butter that had been left too long on a warm stove. Then he pressed the back of her head against the hard plane of his stomach and began to massage her temples with his fingertips, and it was all Laura could do to keep from melting totally.

"Your chocolate's getting cold," she said in a dreamy whisper, afraid that if he didn't stop soon, she would never want him to stop. Tilting her head back a little farther, she opened her eyes and looked up.

His hands froze, then slid slowly down to her neck as he stared at her. For a long, breathless moment Laura waited, looking into the dark sapphire eyes that searched her to her depths.

She could almost feel the kiss in his gaze. Then, with a slow reluctance, his hands moved down her neck to her shoulders, and he stepped back, breaking the slender thread that bound them. His lips brushed over her brow in a fleeting caress before he left her and returned to his chair across the table.

Disappointed almost to the point of tears, Laura kicked herself mentally as she took a big gulp of lukewarm chocolate. When he did try to kiss her, she didn't want him to. Then when he didn't try to kiss her, she wished that he had. And pecks on the forehead didn't count.

She stared dismally at the frothy white mound of melted marshmallows that floated in her mug and longed for the carefree days of youth when a kiss was just a kiss and life wasn't nearly so complicated.

"What about the other story?" Houston asked in a voice more raspy than normal.

Laura looked up from the depths of her cocoa and answered blankly, "What?"

"You were supposed to tell me how you ended up in the ditch."

"Oh." She studied her mug while she tried to clear her mind.

His hair was drying, and a few wavy strands had fallen over his forehead just above his left eye. The image lingered in front of her as she reminded herself that this was the wrong time and that he would be the wrong man at any time. There was no denying that Houston was a man who had a lot to offer, but he was going to have to offer it to some other woman.

"Laura?"

"Yes?" She looked up.

"The ditch?"

"Oh," she said. She struggled to pull her thoughts together.

"You'd been crying," he offered helpfully.

She nodded. "I couldn't see the road."

"Normally when people can't see the road, they slow down." Houston shifted restlessly in his chair, trying to keep his voice to a low growl. The sudden flash of anger that burned inside him was out of place, and he knew it. "You were driving like a bat out of hell."

She spread her hands helplessly. "I don't remember driving that fast."

"You could have killed yourself, Laura." His anger evaporated as suddenly as it had come, and he ran his finger tenderly across her palm, then folded her hand into his. "Why were you crying?"

She closed her eyes and tried not to remember, but the thoughts came flooding back and the tears were once again rising fast. "Oh, Houston," she begged, "it's so hard."

"And you've had a bad day, I know. But I care, Laura. More than you know, and probably a lot more than you want me to."

She tried to twist her hand out of his, but he just held her tighter, and finally she said, "We didn't hear from Dad for years after we left. Then, after a while, Lorene and I came back for a couple of summers. But it never worked out."

Houston turned his hand on hers until their palms were touching, and without thinking, Laura entwined her fingers with his and squeezed.

"So," she continued after a long breath, "we didn't hear from him for another long time. Lorene decided she hated him, but I still sent cards, for Christmas, Father's Day, like that. Some years he answered. Some years he didn't. Then last spring Etta called."

Laura interrupted herself and concentrated her wandering gaze on Houston. "He had pneumonia, and Etta said he might die."

"He had a cold when I left last spring," Houston said quietly.

"It scared me to death." The tears Laura had been holding back slid from the corners of her eyes and down her cheeks. "I knew that once I got here, I could never leave him again, no matter what. So I sold my business and moved here."

Houston didn't even try to keep the surprise off his face. "You had a business?"

Laura could see his shock and couldn't help smiling in spite of her tears. "You wouldn't think it, but northwest Arkansas is very touristy. And trendy. I owned a couple of tearooms in the area. But . . ." She bit her lower lip and felt the grief engulf her again.

"When I thought I was losing Dad with all those years
of emptiness still between us, nothing else mattered."

Houston sat back, keeping her hand in his, and let
out a long sigh. He had known the situation between
Laura and Max was bad. But he hadn't realized Laura
had given up everything for a reunion that just wasn't
going to happen. At least not without a lot of heartbreak along the way.

"Damn, honey. I'm sorry," he said. Reaching into
his back pocket, he pulled out a pressed and neatly
folded handkerchief and handed it to her.

Laura breathed in the freshly laundered scent as she
dabbed at her tear-streaked cheeks. "I didn't know
people still carried these things," she said with a shaky
smile.

"A few of us old-fashioned ones do." When she
handed him the handkerchief, he shoved it into his
pocket and wished he still held her hand in his. That
one tenuous connection had felt very good to him.

"Actually," she said, returning to her story, "I
think I was crying mostly because I've finally given
up."

"You're leaving?" He remembered Max saying that
she would leave, and he wondered if she knew how
little her father really wanted that.

"Partially. I'm opening a tearoom in Savannah. It'll
get me out of Dad's hair and give me something to do
while I'm waiting to see if I'll ever really have a father
again."

"Laura..." He looked at her and wished with
everything in him that he could make her pain go
away. The pale cream of her skin was flushed with the
lightest shade of pink. And the jade green of her lu-

minous eyes was a little darker than usual. Other than that, there was no trace of the tears that had come and gone so quickly. "Max does love you. He'd rather get lockjaw than say it, but I know he does."

She reached across the table and touched his cheek with her fingertips. He looked so serious, so concerned. "Houston, you're sweet. And I'm sorry you've been drawn into this."

When she started to take her hand away, he caught it in his, and she didn't try to fight. For once, she was content to enjoy the comfort of his touch. "It wasn't until today," she said slowly, "that I finally realized what drove Mother away. It wasn't the anger at all. It was the coldness. Houston, it's so awful to watch someone you love look at you as if you're a stranger."

For a second, Houston closed his eyes against the agony that was so raw in her voice. He wasn't so sure anymore that he should have coaxed her into talking about it. He wasn't so sure about a lot of things anymore, except the way he felt about Laura. Simple physical passion had given way to something much deeper, and that wasn't going to make either of their lives any easier.

"It was a polo accident, wasn't it?" he asked with something approaching dread.

She nodded, catching her bottom lip between her teeth to keep it from trembling.

"I guess you think I was a little out of line today when I tried to convince you that polo was harmless."

Laura looked at him with a sharpened awareness. Somewhere the conversation had shifted, and she knew they weren't just talking about her father. "My life would have been a lot different if the horse that tried to step over Dad hadn't stepped on him, instead.''

"I know you can't help the way you feel," he said, almost pleading, "but neither can I. I love it. I love the excitement of it. The danger of it. All of it. I feel alive when I'm out there."

Without any sign of emotion, Laura said, "I was there when it happened." And for as long as she lived she would never forget the sight of her father's still body on that huge grassy field—or the year of heartache that followed—or the day her mother had finally given up the fight to keep their family together.

"It could happen to anyone," she continued with the same steely lack of emotion. "And I will never go through that again."

"It will never happen to me." He offered it as a promise, but Laura held her lower lip between her teeth and shook her head.

"I can't help the way I feel," she said simply.

"Neither can I."

Houston brought her hand to his lips and kissed her palm as a peace offering. "I'd like to hear about your tearoom," he said when he let her hand go, "the one you're planning to open in Savannah."

Grateful for the change of subject, Laura couldn't hide her enthusiasm for her plans. "It's a terrible old place on River Street."

"One of those warehouses?"

She nodded, and Houston groaned inside. As a tourist, River Street was one of his favorite places to wander. But those buildings were ancient, and he could just imagine what an empty one looked like inside.

"I suppose you're going to have to do a lot of renovating," he said, careful to keep his voice neutral.

"You can't imagine."

"Yes, I can." He smiled a little reluctantly. He might end up regretting it later, but he knew what he was going to do. "You've never asked me what I do for a living, have you?"

"I thought you were a rancher."

"My father's a rancher. My older brother and I own a construction company in Dallas."

Laura was stunned as images of skyscrapers leaped into her head. Anyone who watched television knew what the Dallas skyline looked like. Even if her vision wasn't accurate, she couldn't help being impressed. "My goodness," she whispered.

"I know a little bit about renovation. Have you had someone look at the place yet?"

She shook her head, afraid to hope that he was about to say what she thought he was about to say.

"Do you have a pretty good idea of what you want to do?" he asked.

"I know exactly what I want to do," she said quickly.

"Great. Tomorrow we'll get your car out of the ditch, and while somebody checks it over, I'll take you into Savannah for a look at your new business."

A feather could have flattened her. It was all she could do to keep from grabbing him and kissing him. "Houston, I don't know what to say."

"Let's say good night," he answered lightly. "We've got a lot to do tomorrow."

They left the kitchen in a mess that would start Etta's day with a headache, and Houston walked Laura to her door in companionable silence. Once there, he paused, and for a dizzying moment Laura was sure he was about to take her in his arms.

A stillness came over him as he rested his forearm on the door frame above her head.

"I . . ." He paused and tilted his head to stare at the ceiling while he drew in a deep breath.

Laura waited, her heart in her throat. He was going to kiss her. She could feel it all the way through her.

He lowered his head and cupped her chin in his free hand, lifting her face to his. The look in his eyes simmered with desire, and his voice whispered to her with an almost haunting sadness. "I want you, Laura." His thumb gently stroked the edge of her mouth. "I know it's too soon. I know all the reasons you think it couldn't work. But I can't help the way I feel. I don't want to say good night to you. I don't want to go to my room and sleep alone."

She hadn't realized how much she wanted him until she tried to say no. The word wouldn't come. She stared at him with her lips parted. Her heart pounded in her ears, keeping time with the pulsing that started low in her stomach and spread down her legs.

She couldn't do what he asked. She wouldn't. But she couldn't bring herself to say no, either. She stood there, surrounded by him, and stared at him, her eyes wide and eloquent with the agony of her decision.

He didn't move. The muscles of his clenched jaw stood out against the taut pull of his suddenly pale cheeks, and slowly the hand that held her chin dropped to his side.

"I had to ask," he said quietly. "If you change your mind, you know where my room is."

He turned and started to walk away before Laura found her voice. "Aren't you going to..." Her sentence trailed off, and he stopped and looked at her questioningly.

"Going to what?"

He seemed distant, as if he had already gone and she was seeing nothing more than a lingering image. "Kiss me good night?" she finished in a breathless whisper.

"I think it would be best if I didn't try to touch you right now." He gave her a crooked smile that looked anything but happy. "It's taking everything I've got to walk away, Laura. Don't make it any harder, please."

He was so still. So calm. It was hard for her to believe the current of supercharged tension that crackled in the air between them.

"I'm sorry." It sounded so feeble, but she couldn't think of anything else to say.

"Don't be. You're not ready. I am." He shrugged and almost succeeded with a real smile. "Tomorrow's another day, and I'm a patient man. Now go to bed before I change my mind."

Wordlessly, Laura kissed the tips of her first two fingers and turned them toward him in parting before she slipped through her doorway. Inside, she leaned against the closed door and tried to calm the riot of her emotions.

All she had expected was a kiss. A simple kiss. She could have handled that. She'd even reached the point where she wanted it. When she thought of their kiss on horseback, her panic was gone, and a low, slow-burning fire had taken its place. And when she imagined his arms closing around her and his lips covering hers, the flames leaped to a full blaze.

But what she hadn't expected was a blunt proposition. It was more than she wanted and more than she could handle. It was more than she was willing to think about.

When she took off her robe and slipped into bed, she wondered what there was about darkness that made impossible things seem so easy. Was it loneliness that made her feel such a tug on her heart? Or was it just the darkness that made her wish for something that could never be?

Tomorrow Houston would give her his professional advice, and then in a few days he would go to Texas to resume a life that had nothing to do with her. Laura punched her pillow with her fist and burrowed under the covers. If he was lucky, he would live a long and healthy life. If he wasn't, she would never know, and in time she would forget they had ever met.

A sudden gust of wind rattled the windowpanes and hurled rain against the side of the house. Laura snuggled deeper under her comforter. It was going to be a long, cold winter, but at the end of it a new life was waiting for her.

Chapter Five

The quiet sound Houston made deep in his throat wasn't exactly a groan, but it was close enough to worry Laura. The second floor of the property she wanted to lease didn't look any better in the sunshine than it had in the gloom of the previous day.

"What did you want to put in here?" Houston asked as noncommittally as he could.

Laura looked around the tattered room and slowly recreated it the way she knew it could be, with the old wood floor scrubbed and polished. Wooden barrels of imported coffee beans would line the brick wall at the back, and crocks filled with teas from around the world would scent the air. From the exposed ceiling beams, she could hang brass kitchenware, hand-crafted baskets and bunches of dried flowers and herbs. Pleased with the picture, she couldn't help smiling.

"This would be the shop with the coffee and tea. I don't want to change it much. Just clean it up and put in a counter and some shelves. I want to make it homey and rustic."

"Rustic, you've got," Houston said, looking around him. "Homey may take some work."

Laura cheerfully ignored his skepticism and turned to look at the wall that separated this room from the adjacent identical one. "And I'd like to take out part of that wall and put in a set of French doors. That room I want to decorate like a breakfast nook where people can buy one-cup samples of the coffee and tea along with pastries and maybe biscuits or bagels."

"Let's go take a look at it."

Laura led him across the hallway and into the opposite room, which looked at least as bad as the one they had just left. Going to one of the two windows at the front of the room, she kicked aside some debris and stooped to look at the floor. "Don't you think with some sanding and polishing this floor will be okay?"

"Bare?" The horror he carefully schooled out of his voice shone naked from his eyes.

"It looks like pine to me. What do you think? Pine has such a nice golden glow. So cheerful." Laura looked at him. She was rapidly coming to the conclusion that while he might be competent as a builder, he had little or no vision as a decorator. "I'll want these walls papered. I'm not sure about the ceiling in here, but I definitely want bare beams in the other room."

Houston lowered himself to a squat beside her and stared at the patch of flooring she had cleared. It could easily have been a century since it had been cleaned. "You sure there isn't another place you could lease?"

"Not for this money. Besides, this one's perfect."

"It's going to cost you a fortune to renovate." He lifted his eyes from the filthy, scarred floor to her hopeful pale green gaze. "It'd be a lot better to go over this with soap and water and put down carpeting."

Laura shook her head stubbornly. "I'm just not a carpet person. And neither are the kind of people who'll be coming here."

"You're pretty sure of yourself."

"I've had this kind of place before. I'm not just opening a specialty shop on River Street. I'm offering people a sense of history. A place with character. And you don't cover that up with carpeting."

Her last words rang with an almost missionary zeal, and Houston smiled slowly, his grin growing broader until he broke into a quiet chuckle. "Sorry," he said tenderly, and touched the tip of her slender, elegant nose with his finger. "Why didn't you just tell me how much this place means to you?"

Flustered, as she always was when Houston seemed suddenly to see the heart of her, Laura stood abruptly and started toward the door. Halfway across the room, she stopped and turned to face him from a safe distance. "Do you want to see the upstairs?"

Without answering, Houston rose and followed her. On the staircase, barely a step behind her, he said, "You're kind of sensitive today, aren't you?"

Laura didn't know what to say, so she didn't say anything. She hadn't meant to bolt like that, but

Houston had a way of making her nervous. She realized he was doing her a favor by being there, and the last thing she wanted to do was to offend him.

In fact, he'd done her a lot of favors in the short time she had known him. Maybe that was a big part of what made her so nervous. He made it too easy for her to lean on him. Too painless for her to shift just a little of her burden onto his broad shoulders.

"So, when do you think I might expect you to speak to me again?" Houston asked, interrupting her roaming thoughts.

Laura didn't know if he had intended to amuse her or just halt her wandering mind, but she ended up wanting to laugh. "Any minute now," she said with a slow smile.

"Good. The silence was getting to me."

She turned and faced him as he stepped onto the landing at the top of the stairs. He scared her; he annoyed her; he charmed her. But right now he mostly made her feel a little silly for her abrupt exit downstairs. "I feel just the tiniest little urge to apologize," she confessed.

"I'm overwhelmed." He regarded her with dark, unsmiling eyes. "But you really don't have to. I'm starting to get used to those walls you keep throwing up."

Despite his grave expression, Laura was having a little trouble taking him seriously. "Honestly, Houston. Which misguided person ever led you to think you were a patient man?"

Houston leaned against the wall and leisurely crossed his arms over his chest. "You're trying to tell me something, right?"

"Only that you probably wouldn't run into so many walls if you went just a little slower," she said. "After all, we *are* practically strangers."

He stiffened and arched one brow in warning. "Funny, but after last night I find it a little hard to think of you as a stranger." His words had a husky undertone that added volumes to the hard glint in his eyes.

Suddenly self-conscious, Laura shrugged and casually tilted her head to examine the ceiling. The last thing she wanted to think about at the moment was what had happened, or could have happened, between them the night before. The feelings he had touched were still too close to the surface.

She lowered her eyes finally, only to discover that the storm in his blue gaze had intensified. She hesitated, looking away again. "Maybe that's part of the problem. Maybe we just went a little too far too fast."

"We?" he challenged. "You mean me, don't you?"

If she could have, she'd have curled into a tight little ball and rolled into a corner to hide. She hadn't been ready to have him make love to her last night, and she wasn't ready to have an argument about it now. "You weren't alone," she said in a voice just above a whisper.

"I'm feeling pretty alone right now."

"Well, you're not." Feeling trapped and angry, she looked into his eyes for one intense moment, then walked past him into the space she hoped to make into a tearoom.

She didn't know what he wanted from her. It was obviously more than friendship, but how much more she didn't want to find out. Couldn't he see how dan-

gerous he was for her? Didn't he know he was everything she didn't want? And if it was an affair he was
after, he was out of his mind if he thought she was ever
going to agree.

"You know, eventually we're going to get back to
this subject," Houston said quietly, a few steps behind her.

"Fine," she answered in a stiff tone that was just a
shade nicer than curt. "Let's worry about it then."

She stood in the middle of what had been a living
room and tried to put aside the tension between them.
Facing the three full-length windows at the front of the
room, she held out her arms. "Well, what do you
think?"

Houston's breath escaped in a slow hiss. When he
answered, his tone of voice was businesslike. "What's
this going to be?"

"The tearoom. Baked goods for breakfast. Soups,
salads, sandwiches and desserts for lunch. Open beam
ceiling with hanging plants."

"Wood floor," Houston supplied.

Laura turned and smiled. "Wood floor," she
agreed, and gestured behind him. "With a counter
there. An antique one, if I can find it. There's already
a kitchen in the back, but it'll have to be totally redone to handle a restaurant. There's a place across the
hall that can be used as a storeroom and several bath-
rooms that could be enlarged for the public. This looks
better than the downstairs, doesn't it?"

"At first glance," he said cautiously. "I'll still have
to check it out structurally. Is this it?" Houston
looked around him, but his expression gave nothing
away.

"One more thing."

The slight hesitation in her voice alerted him, and Laura didn't like the glimmer she saw leap into his eyes. "An apartment," she added, and didn't wait for his reaction before she led him across the landing and into a small alcove. When she saw he was following, she opened the door and went through.

It was a large room, with three tall windows that matched those in the room they had just left, but without the balcony. A small, sad-looking bathroom was just behind the door, and at the opposite end of the main room was a kitchenette that appeared unsalvageable. The long wall that extended from the entrance to the kitchenette was brick. Both the brick wall and the wooden planks of the floor showed the scars of dividing walls that had been put in then torn out again.

"What's this for?" Houston asked with the barest trace of hostility.

"I've got to live somewhere."

"No. Absolutely not," he said heatedly, abandoning all pretense of keeping a polite distance from her private life. "This whole thing is a bad idea. It's bad enough that you want to turn this trash heap into a place where innocent people will come to eat, but to try to live here? No way. I won't allow it."

His open display of possession shocked them both into a long moment of silence. When the full meaning of his outburst finally registered, a hot flash of anger swept through Laura.

"You won't what?" she asked.

Knowing instantly that he had gone too far, Houston swallowed his pride and tried to retreat. "I shouldn't have said that. I can't say I didn't mean it, but I shouldn't have said it.''

"You won't allow it?'' Laura repeated with deadly calm. Her hands on her hips and challenge in her eyes, she watched him. She had made it to the age of twenty-six without having anybody run her life for her, and she intended to keep it that way.

He frowned and stood a little straighter. Retreat was impossible, so he plunged blindly ahead. "It's my professional opinion that this place will never be habitable.''

"That's a crock, and you know it.'' Seeing his obvious discomfort displayed so openly on his handsome face, Laura found that her anger was slipping away, and she resented it deeply.

"I don't want you living here,'' Houston insisted.

"People live all along here.'' She flung out her arm to include Factor's Walk, the historic district and a sizable chunk of Savannah.

"I don't want *you* living here,'' Houston insisted loudly.

Deciding the most dignified course of action would be to drop the argument entirely, Laura said, "It would be nice if the bathroom could be enlarged, but if it's not possible, I could survive. The kitchenette would have to be redone, and while we're at it, we might as well put in a partition and turn it into a real kitchen. I don't think I want any other walls put in, though. I like it open.''

She gestured to the boarded-up windows. "With those windows replaced, the view of the river will be wonderful, especially at night. I could design the whole room around that view.''

Subdued, Houston asked quietly, "You're going to do this anyway, aren't you?"

Laura turned from the windows and faced him with determination in every line of her body. She didn't now why she wanted this particular place so much, but she did. And the more impossible the whole thing seemed, the more determined she became. "I'm going to do this."

"Then I guess I'll have to help you," he said, knowing when to give up on a lost battle.

Stunned, she knew she must have misunderstood him. "What do you mean? Help me how?"

"You need a contractor." He shrugged slightly and tapped himself on the chest. "I'm a contractor."

Laura shook her head slowly. "You're a Dallas contractor. This is Savannah." Then, beginning to recover from her shock, she added hastily, "It's not that I don't appreciate your offer, but I need somebody who's going to be here. This job's going to take at least six months, and I'm going to be too busy finding suppliers for the shop and taking care of the decor to deal with the renovation."

"I'll be here," he said simply.

"How?"

"Let me work that out." Houston lifted a brow quizzically, still uncertain if she was going to accept his offer. "So, do we have a deal?"

"You haven't asked about the financing," she hedged.

"I hope you've got plenty of it, because what you want to do isn't going to be cheap."

"I honestly don't know, Houston." Grateful for someone she could talk to honestly about the problems she faced, Laura felt her anxiety pouring onto Houston's broad shoulders. "I can't tell you how many nights I've lain awake wondering if I can pull this off. I've got the paperwork in the car."

"You hungry?"

She thought about it for a minute and realized that she was. "Ravenous."

He slid his arm around her waist and turned her toward the door. "Let's do the math on a full stomach."

"Great."

Almost dazed by his generous offer, she couldn't help feeling that her relief was a little too intense. She reminded herself that Houston was too easy to like, too easy to lean on. But she needed a contractor, and while his arm was around her, she couldn't help believing that he really could make a difference. And more than anything else, she needed this tearoom.

If he started getting too close, she could handle it. Their relationship would be strictly business. Friendly, but nothing more. Even Houston would understand that was how it would have to be. It just wouldn't work any other way.

Houston shuffled the papers in front of him one more time. He was glad he had eaten first, because he didn't know how he could have explained his sudden loss of appetite to Laura. He stole a furtive glance in her direction, and the glance grew into a lingering study.

She sat on the iron railing that separated the wide brick walkway from the river a few feet below. A small flock of sea gulls gathered on the sidewalk in front of her, scurrying for the popcorn she tossed out by the handful. The thick waves of her dark blond hair caught the light and shimmered like molten gold in the sun.

Without makeup her face had a childlike piquancy. But with the subtle strokes of shadow and light that she wore now, she became a woman—exotic, elegant . . . and as fragile as an orchid.

As if she read his mind, Laura lifted her wide, sloping cat-green eyes to his. A pale pink gloss heightened the delicate fullness of her mouth. Her lips slowly parted in a smile, and Houston felt his heart skip a beat while he wondered how he could tell her that she didn't have enough money.

Lifting a slender, honey-bronzed arm, she tossed a fat kernel of popcorn straight at him. Houston opened his mouth and reached for it, but it hit the tip of his chin and bounced off. Still smiling, Laura slid an even fatter piece between her parted white teeth and chewed with exaggerated slowness. And in that moment, no power on earth could have forced him to give her bad news.

Without looking away from her, Houston stuffed the papers scattered around him into the briefcase he had taken them from and left the messy result on the bench. She tossed another piece of popcorn at him while he was rising, and he caught it with his hand.

"No fair!" Laura laughed. She hurled a series of fluffy white missiles at him while he advanced steadily, and he batted them at her with his open palm. As he got nearer, and the return lobs came faster, she turned to the side after each toss and finally covered her head with her arm in defense. When he rushed at her across the last few feet, she screeched and almost dropped the popcorn bag.

Houston caught the bag with one hand and scooped her against him with the other. As she threw back her head and looked at him with laughter shining in her eyes, he cautioned himself that it was impossible to fall in love in a day. But his emotions shouted that that was exactly what he had done, and his instincts told him that he held in his arms the woman he could be happy with for the rest of his life.

And if he kissed her now, he would ruin it all. The laughter would die, and the shutters would close against emotions she couldn't accept. Pretending a patience he didn't feel and giving her the space she needed would be the hardest things he had ever done. But if he wanted her, that was the way it would have to be.

"What do you think?" she asked, contentedly standing in the circle of his arm.

Unwilling to do anything to disturb the happiness that shimmered in her eyes, Houston was careful not to say the first thing that popped into his mind. "About what?" he asked cautiously.

Laura looked at him as if he were a lovable dunce. "The financing. Is it going to work?"

He took a deep breath and smiled at her. If he had to finance the damned thing himself, she was going to get what she wanted. "We'll see if we can get the owner to bring down his price and kick in a little more with the renovation. And we'll see if the bank will go just a little higher."

Suddenly serious, she asked, "It's going to be a tight squeeze, isn't it?"

"You've got a residence combining with two separate businesses. That increases your overhead without increasing your revenue potential. And the first year in any new business is always a bitch. Banks don't like to think of themselves as charity institutions."

She ran her hand absentmindedly over her stomach, and he knew that reality was having the same effect on her appetite as it had had on his. "Hey," he crooned softly. When she lifted her eyes to his, her forlorn expression cut him like a knife. "We can do it." He put his heart into his words, and his eyes begged her to believe him.

"We can?" she asked without a great deal of faith.

"If you'll trust me. Just tell me what you want, and let me take care of it. I can get you a better price across the board than what you can get for yourself."

"Who'll handle the money?"

"Joint account. But I'd rather write the checks, since I'll be spending most of the money."

He could feel her withdrawing into herself. He waited, knowing that he asked a lot. And when she finally came back to him, he could see a calmness in her that hadn't been there before, and with it a trust that captured his heart forever.

"I would never betray you, Laura," he promised.

"I know," she said softly. "You're a very noble man." She smiled a small, teasing smile. "Code of the West and all that."

Realizing that her assessment was embarrassingly close to the mark, Houston felt a moment of discomfort before he chuckled. "You're going to have to stop making fun of me, young lady."

"I'm sorry," she said contritely, but her grin continued to hold the sparkle of mischief. "It's just that sometimes you're such a perfect white knight, I have trouble taking you seriously."

He resisted kissing her, but just barely, and the longing was heavy in his voice when he said softly, "But I like rescuing you."

She looked into his eyes for the breadth of a heartbeat. "You do it so well."

A gentle smile tugged at the corners of his mouth. "And you need it so often."

She laughed. "Just don't get tired of it before we get this thing finished."

"I don't think there's any danger of that."

Sometime during their conversation, her hand had slid beneath his arm and around his waist. Her other palm rested lightly on his chest. He slowly tightened his arm on her back and gently pulled her nearer. The parted invitation of her smiling lips was temptingly near.

"Ah, Ms. Warner, there you are," a woman's voice called eagerly.

Houston clenched his teeth on an angry groan. "*Who* is that?" he asked under his breath.

Laura peered around his shoulder and saw Mrs. Sanderson advancing toward them. "The realtor," she whispered. "We still have her key."

"I'll take it from here," he said. Wanting nothing more than to get rid of the woman, he smoothed out the scowl that had gathered on his brow and turned to face the smiling, robust lady who stopped a few feet in front of them. "How do you do, ma'am." He held out his hand and clasped hers warmly. "I'm Houston

Carder. I'll be Ms. Warner's general contractor on this project. Do you have the authority to negotiate for the owner?''

"Belle Sanderson," the woman supplied as she pumped his hand. Answering his question, she said, "To a point. Is there a problem?"

"If you don't mind," he said, bypassing her question, "I'd like to keep the key another day and do a more thorough study of the property tomorrow. Then I'd like to discuss a few things with you."

Knowing a dismissal when she got one, Mrs. Sanderson took a step back. "I'm sure that'll be just fine." She looked at Laura, who smiled and remained silent. The realtor automatically reached into her pocket and pulled out a business card. "My card," she said, handing it to Houston. "Just let me know when you're ready to get together." With a polite nod, she retreated through the parking lot and picked her way carefully across the railroad track that ran down the middle of River Street.

"Efficient little fellow, aren't you?" Laura asked when the older lady was out of earshot.

Their earlier mood broken, he hooked his arm around her waist again and guided her toward the briefcase on the bench, then to the parking lot where his car waited. "I always like to impress the boss right off, so I don't have to worry about it once I get down to work."

"Well, I'm impressed."

"Good. With a little more work, you might even begin to take me seriously." He tried not to think of how close he had come to making love to her on the sidewalk of a busy tourist area.

"There's always that possibility."

Laura smiled as she spoke, but he thought he heard the faintest echo of worry. He had six months to get past the barriers she had built around her heart, and Houston thought he might have detected the first crack in the wall.

By the time the renovation was ending, it would be springtime. And he'd seen Savannah in the spring. It was a city made for lovers, and a season perfect for wooing. If he couldn't make her love him by then, he knew he never would.

"Jack?"

"Houston," the voice rumbled out of the receiver with the flawless clarity of modern technology. An edge of alarm strengthened its carrying power. "What's wrong?"

"Nothing's wrong," Houston said. He slid deeper into his chair and propped his feet, boots and all, on the edge of the bed. "Why should anything be wrong?"

"Why are you calling?" his brother asked with confusion.

"Just wanted to see how business was going," Houston answered with exaggerated ease.

"You've only been gone three days. What did you think was going to happen?"

"Well, you know, I like to stay in touch."

"Since when?" Jack laughed and gave up trying to force an answer out of Houston. After thirty-three years, if he had learned anything, it was when to give up trying to pull information out of his younger brother.

"Heard anything on the Caitlin bid?" Houston slunk a little lower in his chair and tried to pretend he was relaxed. Maybe he should have waited until later to call. He might have caught Jack when he was sleepier and a little less suspicious.

"Yeah. We didn't get it. Cooperman underbid us again. He's using either second-grade materials or slave labor."

"Well," Houston drawled, "maybe it's for the best." Ordinarily he would have felt the same disgust he heard in his brother's voice, but at the moment the loss of the job was going to make his news a little easier to take.

"You fall off one of those polo ponies onto your head, son?" Jack snapped. "Losing business is never for the best."

"It is when I'm going to be working on a job in Savannah through the winter," Houston said softly.

There was dead silence on the other end of the line, then, "Say again?"

"I'm going to be working on a renovation here that will probably take till spring."

"Bull. You haven't done a renovation since you were a kid. We can't make any money on a renovation. Are you out of your mind?"

Houston could tell that Jack was just getting warmed up, so he plunged ahead when his brother stopped for breath. "It's not for profit. It's a favor." Knowing what was probably coming next, he held the receiver a few inches away.

"A favor!"

The words blasted in his ear, and after a safe pause Houston brought the receiver close again. "We can afford it," he said calmly. "Alan can fill in for me there. He's ready for more responsibility anyway."

"He's barely out of college. He's not a partner, and it's not fair to ask him to do your job," Jack argued.

"He's our brother, and he's already said he wants to come into the business. All he needs is experience."

"He'll get his experience from the bottom up, Houston. The way we did. He's not going to start out filling the shoes you wear now, so leave him out of this."

"Fine," Houston said. He didn't like it, but he realized Jack was right. Alan wasn't ready, and it wouldn't be right to push him too fast.

Sighing audibly, Houston started over again. "Jack, look, I know this is a hardship. And I'm sorry. But it's something I've got to do. Can you find some way to work around me for the next six months?"

"Is this about that ranch you're trying to buy there?"

"No, not really." He wished Jack would stop prying. Having a protective big brother was great when you were young, and not so great when you were grown and trying to live your own life.

"Is it a woman?"

Houston jumped as if he'd been stuck by a pin. "For crying out loud, Jack, would you drop it?" In his mind, he could see Jack nodding wisely, preparing his latest piece of unwanted advice.

"That's it, isn't it? You've been there, what, a day, two days? Houston, you've got to get over this Sir Galahad complex. Leave one or two distressed damsels for the next guy. Now I suppose you're going to tell me this one's special."

More than mildly irritated, Houston sat up straight and put his feet on the floor. "She is."

"Oh, man, where have I heard that one before?"

"I don't need this grief, Jack," Houston said through clenched teeth.

"And I don't need you skipping out on the half dozen jobs you're in charge of for a woman you couldn't have known more than two days. For the next six months you're going to be getting your half of the company's profits while I'm the one who's doing all the work. And that, brother mine, is grief *I* don't need."

"Well, in that case, why wait until I've bought this ranch here?" Houston said, stiffening with anger. "Buy me out now. I'll be home for Thanksgiving, and we can work out the details."

Silence stretched across the long-distance wires once more, and when Jack spoke again, it was quietly. "So, how special is this lady?"

Instantly Houston relaxed, glad for the ear of the older brother who had guided him into manhood. "If I can manage to make her love me," he said, "I think I'm going to marry her."

Jack whistled softly. "Who is she?"

"Maxwell Warner's daughter."

"Hm," Jack said, and Houston could almost hear him sitting back, thinking. "I didn't know Max had a daughter."

"Two daughters. Their mother took them and left after Max had his accident."

"Damned decent of her," Jack said dryly.

"There are two sides to every story. Max isn't so easy to live with." Houston couldn't help thinking of the tears he had seen Laura shed, of her wreck, which could have been so much worse, of the cold, proud distance Max kept between himself and his daughter.

"Is your new love just visiting, or does she live there now?"

"She came back here to live, but it's not working out. I'm going to be renovating a business and apartment for her in Savannah."

The cautious, brotherly probing shifted to a more professional tone. "What kind of business?"

"Some kind of a restaurant and coffee shop. She calls it a tearoom."

"Is this a hobby you're helping her with, or is she actually going to be able to make a living at this?" Jack asked skeptically.

Houston shook his head in wonder. "She owned two of them in Arkansas before she came here." In theory he agreed with his brother. He didn't see how anybody could make a living selling specialty coffees and cute sandwiches. "She obviously knows what she's doing. But I'll be damned if I know how she makes it work."

"Is she pretty?"

"She's a little doll. Blond hair. Green eyes. And a body—" He stopped abruptly. Even to himself, Houston thought he sounded like a lovesick sap, but he couldn't help it. And the longer he knew her, the harder it became to hold on to the little control he had left.

"Careful, son," Jack cautioned. Even through the distance, he could hear things in his brother's voice he had never heard before. "This one sounds like it could be serious."

"It scares the hell out of me, I'll tell you that," Houston agreed. He still got cold chills when he remembered his reaction to the dangerous combination of the beautiful baby face and ripe woman's body that greeted him the first time he saw Laura.

"You going to bring her home with you at Thanksgiving?"

"Are you kidding? If she had any idea I was this serious, she'd run the other way so fast I'd never catch her."

Sliding back into business for a moment, Jack asked, "Are you going to charge her for this renovation?"

"She thinks I am." Houston drew in a deep breath and let it out again slowly. He sounded as strained as he felt. "But the truth is, she hasn't got the money to pay me. So I'm going to handle the books to keep her from finding out I'm working for free."

"Oh, Houston, Houston." Jack sighed. "You're getting in deep, boy, and it worries me. I don't want to see you here next spring with a broken heart."

"No promises, Jack. This one's going to be touch and go all the way." Houston rubbed his hand over his neck, automatically probing the tense muscles he found there. It had been a long time since he had felt this alone. He hated to say goodbye. "Kiss Susan and the kids for me. Tell them I'll see them week after next."

"Is there something you're not telling me, Houston?"

Houston heard the concern in Jack's voice, and the temptation to tell him the whole story was strong, but that wouldn't solve anything. The doubts that haunted his future with Laura would still be there.

More than anything he wanted the kind of life his brother had—a happy family and a woman he loved. Houston knew he had found that woman, but she had made it abundantly clear that Houston Carder was the last man on earth she intended to get serious about.

"You're a lucky man, Jack. See you at Thanksgiving."

Longing twisted in the pit of Houston's stomach like the cold, hard grip of a clenched fist. It was there when he hung up without waiting for his brother's goodbye, and it stayed there for a long time afterward.

Chapter Six

Laura stood in the foyer with her back against the newel post. The rich, juicy smells of Thanksgiving hung in the air around her while she listened to the hollow ringing of the telephone she held to her ear and watched the soft, Oriental pattern of the wallpaper opposite her slowly begin to blur.

She tried to fight the sinking feeling in the pit of her stomach, but she knew that if someone didn't answer soon, she was going to cry. She was about to give up hope when the ringing stopped and a sweet, breathless voice at the other end answered, "Hello?"

"Mama?"

"Laura! Darling!" Julia Warner cried in surprise. "How are you? Happy Thanksgiving, sweetheart!"

Suddenly speechless from the overwhelming wave of homesickness that washed over her, Laura clutched

the phone tighter and took a deep breath to steady
herself.

"Happy Thanksgiving to you, too," she said finally in tones cramped with emotion. "How is everybody?"

"Oh, just fine, baby. Lorene and Billy are here, and
we really miss you. Gran and Gramps send their love.
I was going to call you this evening, sweetheart, because you'll never guess what's happened. I just wish
I could see your face when you hear this." Julia
paused for effect, then said in a bubbly rush, "You're
going to be an aunt."

Laura laughed out loud with happy surprise.
"That's great," she cried. Then her smile began to
fade as the loneliness came rushing back, a deep and
aching loneliness for the family she had left behind in
Arkansas.

"Wow. Lorene's pregnant," she said a little un-
evenly and slumped against the newel post. "After all
these years of trying. That's so wonderful."

"Now, sweetheart," her mother coaxed, "don't
cry."

"I can't help it," she answered with tears in her
voice. "It's just so wonderful."

"Laura, are you unhappy? You sound exactly like
you did when you were sixteen and tried to spend
Christmas alone with your father. Where's Etta?"

Laura sniffed and struggled to blink back her tears.
"Etta's visiting her family." She walked around the
newel post and sat on the staircase. "Mom, tell Lorene how happy I am for her and Billy."

"I will, honey," Julia assured her absentmindedly, then turned the subject to Laura. "Where's your father?"

"At the paddock the last time I saw him. Dinner's been ready for an hour, but I can't get him to come in."

"You might try hitting him over the head with a two-by-four and dragging him," her mother suggested sweetly.

"Oh, Mom," Laura said, her tears forgotten as she laughed at the tempting idea. "If I thought it would work, I might try it."

"Well, I can promise you one thing. This is the last holiday you'll spend alone with that man. If you don't come here for Christmas, I'm going to come there." Julia's indignation suddenly dissolved into mischievous laughter. "Boy, would that make him mad."

"Now, Mother," Laura cautioned while visions of famous fights past swam into her head.

Blithely sweeping aside her daughter's protest, Julia said, "Don't 'now, Mother' me, dear. If I want to irritate your father, I have every right. After all, we are still married, and maybe it's about time I gave him a little reminder of it."

Laura closed her eyes and groaned. Her beautiful, spirited mother and her stubborn, embittered father had barely spoken in the fourteen years since they had parted. But when they did, it was far from the cold silence that had led to their split.

Then softly her mother said, "Something has to work, Laura. I just can't stop believing that someday something will work, and Max'll be the way he used to be."

Stunned, Laura slowly opened her eyes at the mingled agony and hope in her mother's voice. It was a mixture she easily recognized because she had heard it so many times in her own voice. "Good grief, Mother," she said quietly. "You still love him."

"Of course, I still love him. You didn't know that?"

"No! You never said it."

"But I never divorced him," Julia said in surprise. "I never dated anyone else. I just thought you knew."

Laughing through the tears that had once more seeped into her eyes, Laura said, "Mom, you never stop amazing me. Did I remember to tell you how much I love you?"

"You're going to make me cry, dear."

Laura laughed again. "Don't do that."

"I think it's too late." Julia sniffed delicately. "I love you, too, baby. Will you take care of that old goat for me?"

"I'll do my best. But he isn't very cooperative."

"Well, you just do what you can. And if you see me before Christmas, don't be too surprised. I think we're overdue for a nice, long, woman-to-woman chat." She sighed. "Does that sound as good to you as it does to me?"

"I have so much to tell you," Laura said, hating to say goodbye.

"I'll be there soon. Say hi to Etta for me, and tell her to get a room ready. But let's not tell your father."

"Oh, my goodness. This is going to be some Christmas."

"Till then, sweetheart."

With that, her mother was gone, and so was the gloom that had threatened the spirit of the day. Feeling more cheerful than she had since Houston's departure a week earlier, Laura went once more in search of her father, determined to salvage what was left of their Thanksgiving Day.

Outside, a stiff wind blew at her back. The sun played hide-and-seek among low-hanging clouds, giving the day a grainy, gray quality. Pulling her flannel shirt tighter around her, Laura clutched a thermos of hot buttered rum in the crook of her arm and started across an empty pasture toward the faint dot that was Max.

Wet, brown leaves clung to her boots as she picked her way across the uneven ground to where he sat huddled in his wheelchair facing a white pipe fence. His back was to her, and as she neared him, Laura could see his head turning to follow the antics of the yearlings in the pasture.

The day was cold and damp, and she worried that Max had been out in it too long already. If the promise of a hot meal couldn't draw him inside, she hoped maybe the thought of a warm fire and good liquor could.

"You haven't come to nag at me some more, have you?" Max grumbled, showing no surprise when she stopped beside him.

"Would it do me any good?"

"No."

"Then I guess I won't."

"What's in that?" he asked, and eyed the thermos with suspicion.

"Your favorite soup," Laura said, unscrewing the lid and pouring him a capful of the steaming liquor.

Max chuckled and took the metal cup she held out to him. "So you still remember that, huh?"

"I don't think I'll ever forget it." Smiling with him, she felt the warm rush of old memories, in particular memories of the cold, wintry days when Max had allowed her to tag along behind him to the stables, each of them carrying a thermos of hot soup. One day, convinced that Max's was better than hers, Laura had quickly gulped down half of his while he wasn't looking, and Max had turned around to find the gasping, red-eyed, nine-year-old Laura spitting out the remnants of the hot buttered rum she hadn't swallowed. Max had had to cut short his day to carry his giggling daughter home.

"Boy, was Mama mad," Laura said with a lingering smile.

Max's face softened, and a faraway look stole into his eyes. "Yeah, she was, wasn't she?"

Then he abruptly snapped closed the shutters that hid his thoughts from the world. "Got any more of that soup?" he asked gruffly, jerking his head toward the thermos.

Pouring another capful, Laura watched him drink half then pass it to her.

"Your turn," he said.

Overhead the gray sky was sagging lower, and the chill wind was growing stiffer. But somehow the day seemed warmer to her as Laura shared a drink with her father.

When the cup was empty, she pointed toward the yearlings. "Nice crop."

The faraway look came into his eyes again, this time coupled with sadness. "They're the future. They're what this place is all about. But they're just babies, and it'll be years before they're ready. Maybe more years than I've got."

Before Laura could react, he wheeled around and headed away from the yearlings as fast as he could go across the uneven ground. Suppressing her urge to help him, Laura caught up and asked, "Where to now?"

"Thought I might give some of that turkey a try. You sure it's cooked all the way? Nothing worse than a half-cooked turkey." He shoved fiercely at the wheels of his chair, propelling himself forward in spurts while his words came out in huffs.

"I owned a restaurant, Dad. I do know how to cook." Trudging along beside him, Laura heard her own voice becoming breathless. "Could we slow down a little?"

"Is there any of that rum left?"

She stopped to pour another capful, and he stopped to wait for it. While they paused, a slow, silent drizzle began to seep from the darkening sky and settle over them in a fine mist.

Max drank half the cup and handed it to her. "Drink up, girl. It's going to be a rotten trip home."

Laura drained the cup and gave him the thermos to hold while she began to wheel the chair toward the house over his indignant protests.

"Once we get there," she said over the noise of his grumbling, "there's a feast waiting in the kitchen, a fire's laid in the dining room, and brandy's on the sideboard."

Sipping at another cup of the hot buttered rum while he tried to sit passively in his wheelchair, Max asked, "Remember the time that old red truck got bogged down, and we ended up hiking through the fields in the rain to get home?"

With the back of her hand, Laura brushed a wet strand of hair out of her eyes. "And it was after dark when we finally got there."

"Way after dark," Max said happily. "How old were you then? Seven?"

"About that."

"Boy, was your mother livid that time."

He sounded so pleased that Laura couldn't help laughing with him. "Poor Mom," she added with real sympathy. "We must have been a trial."

"Yeah, but we had fun, didn't we?"

Max suddenly roared with laughter, and the walk home was finished in a parade of "do you remembers". She had forgotten they had been partners in so much mischief and mishap.

Through dinner they ate and drank and laughed, and late into the night she kissed his brow and helped him to bed. She sat beside him until he was asleep, and still she sat, watching him and wondering how such a wall had come between them where so much love had once been.

Tonight, with the help of rum and memories, they had built a bridge across that wall. Would it stand, she wondered, or would Max awaken with his defenses rebuilt?

And did it really matter? Before Houston left, he had helped her finalize the lease and the loan. The crew he had hired had already begun work.

It was too late to change her plans. Regardless of how she felt today or how Max would feel tomorrow or the day after, she was still committed to leaving, and it was too late to wish that things could be different.

Laura stood in the middle of her would-be apartment and tried not to feel the shock. The kitchenette at one end of the room and the tiny bath at the other end were no longer there. Ugly exposed wall studs, pipes and bare, battered flooring stood as mute reminders that remodeling was only pretty in the end.

"Ah, Miss Warner, glad to see you're wearing that hard hat," boomed a voice that was used to overriding the sounds of construction.

Turning, she watched as Joe Morgan strode into the room and across to the worktable that was set up to hold blueprints.

"Some young blond fellow met me at the door and insisted," Laura said, nervously adjusting the hard yellow hat that was several sizes too big.

"Tony," Joe said, and nodded to the table. "Had a chance to look at these yet?"

"Not really." She edged closer to the huge, dark blue sheets that were spread over every inch of the long table. "Is this everything?"

He touched a cluster at the other end of the table. "Downstairs." Walking toward her, he tapped the pile in the center. "Upstairs." He pointed to the stack of blueprints nearest her. "Apartment."

Laura took an involuntary step back. "I'm not sure I'm really going to understand these."

"Well, so far we're just tearing out and cleaning up. Now I understand that this," he said, indicating the room they were in, "is the first thing you want finished."

Clapping a hand to the top of her head to keep the hat from slipping, Laura nodded.

"Well, I just talked to Houston this morning," he continued, "and it looks like we're gonna have to get started without him. That is, if you're really in a hurry for this place."

"I thought he was supposed to be back next week," she said, feeling a sharp pang of longing at the mention of Houston's name.

"No such luck. He's run into a holdup."

Great, Laura thought. Turning away, she crossed the room and went to stare out the unwashed window at the river. He'd been gone two weeks already, and she hadn't heard a word from him. The foreman had had to tell her that Houston wouldn't be back on schedule, and now she didn't know when he would be back, or how she was supposed to get anything done in the meantime.

For the past week, since that rainy Thanksgiving Day when they had reminisced late into the night, Max had retreated into his own world more than ever. With a new polo clinic starting, he left the house so early and returned so late that Laura was certain he hadn't noticed her absence every day.

"Ahem." Joe cleared his throat loudly, then said, "Uh, excuse me, Miss Warner, but were you going to be needing this apartment soon?"

Laura turned from the window as a tug sounded its deep, lonely horn downriver. "As soon as possible, I'm afraid," she said.

"Want to take a look at the rest of the place while you're here? Then I'll set up a time for us to pick out the fixtures and appliances for in here. Is your schedule flexible the rest of the week?"

"As flexible as they come, Joe. Let's go survey the damage."

For the fourth time in the past fifteen minutes Houston checked his watch and found that the minute hand had crept forward to 5:55 a.m., Dallas time. In another five minutes it would be seven o'clock in Georgia, and he would allow himself to make the call he had been waiting thirty minutes to make.

He toyed with his coffee cup and inched the phone a little closer. Every morning and every evening for two weeks he'd had to struggle against the urge to call Laura, until finally he didn't care anymore if he seemed too eager. He missed her so much that the time away from her had become an agony, and it might be weeks before he could see her again.

Checking his watch once more, he dialed her number two minutes ahead of schedule and listened to the pounding of his heart while he waited to hear the sound of her voice.

Midway through the fourth ring, the receiver at the other end was lifted, then dropped and picked up again. "Hello?" a soft, sleepy voice crooned. "Sorry about that. It slipped."

"Laura?" Houston asked hopefully.

"Houston? Is that you?"

She sounded instantly awake and glad to hear from him.

"If it's too early, I can call back later," he offered. "I didn't mean to get you out of bed."

Laura chuckled. "You didn't."

He could almost hear her snuggle under the covers and his imagination went into overdrive as he pictured what it would be like to wake up next to her every morning. Her hair soft and tousled, caressing her cheek while she slid her head onto his bare shoulder and smiled at him with suggestive mischief in her eyes.

"I talked to Joe yesterday," she said. "He told me you wouldn't be back for a while."

"Yeah, I'm real sorry about that." Reluctantly Houston pulled himself away from his vision of the future to deal with the present. "I should have told you myself. I meant to call you yesterday, but I got tied up, and by the time I was free I was afraid Max would be home. I don't suppose you've told him anything yet."

"No," Laura said with a sigh that made Houston long to comfort her.

"Things aren't going any better?"

"It's no use. I'm just waiting now until my apartment is finished." She sighed again. "I don't think it's going to be very pleasant here once I've told him."

In his heart Houston agreed, but he couldn't help saying, "He might surprise you."

Laura laughed. "Stop trying to make me feel better. Whether he really wants me here or not, Max is going to be furious when he finds out I'm leaving, and you know it."

The more Houston talked to her, the more he missed her and the more guilty he felt for leaving her alone at such a difficult time. "Maybe I could find a few days to get back there. That is, if you really needed me."

"Well, I'm sure Joe's very capable, and I know you must be awfully busy there, but if you had the time…"

Her voice trailed off hopefully, and Houston wished he could catch the next plane. "I can't promise."

"I know you're busy," she said again.

"It's not that. It's…" He found himself wanting to tell her everything, but she had problems enough of her own without hearing his, too. "It's my sister," he said finally. "She's thinking about getting married, and she's staying with me while she makes up her mind."

"So you have to stay there."

"I'll see. It depends on a few things."

Laughing as if she had just thought of something, Laura said, "Well, my mother's coming for a visit. So you might want to call before you come, just to be sure there's still a roof on the place."

"Ouch," Houston said, laughing with her. "Sounds like things have been pretty lively since I left. I guess I'm going to have to call more often."

"That's not such a bad idea." Her voice deepened with a hint of mischief. "I'm sure there'd be lots to talk about."

Houston heaved a sigh and held the phone closer. "We never seem to have a problem there."

"No," she agreed, her tones softening almost to a whisper, "we don't, do we?"

"Would you mind if I called you again in the morning?"

''No. It's a nice way to start the day.''

Before he could agree, Houston heard a toilet flush and the sound of running water. ''I think my house-guest is up,'' he said reluctantly.

''Till tomorrow?'' Laura asked.

''Till tomorrow,'' he promised, and slowly lowered the phone.

She missed him. He could hear it in her voice. He could feel it in the things she'd almost said. She wanted him with her nearly as much as he wanted to be there.

The meandering of his thoughts halted as a sound behind him caught his attention and he turned to find his sister standing in the kitchen doorway. The dark circles under her eyes told him all he needed to know about the kind of night she had had.

She smiled weakly. ''Till tomorrow? Could that have been the fair Laura?''

''Sit down before you faint,'' Houston said, getting up to help her. ''You're too sick to be teasing anybody.''

She trembled in his arms when he led her to the table. ''It'll pass,'' she assured him in a voice that faded to a whisper.

''What do you want to eat?''

The little color she had left drained from her face as he watched. ''Don't say that word,'' she whispered. ''Just milk. And a cracker.''

''Rebecca.''

''Now.''

He brought her a glass of milk and helped her steady it in shaking hands, then he opened a package of crackers and set them in front of her.

"Marry the bastard," he said firmly.

"I'd still be throwing up," she answered with a weak smile.

He sat across from her. "That will get better. Raising a child alone won't."

She shook her head stubbornly. "It would be two mistakes instead of one."

Houston looked at her. Rebecca, his quiet, sweet, sensible sister. The one he never had to worry about. The one who had always known when he had needed someone to lean on.

To see her now in such need and to be able to do so little to help was almost more than he could take. He wanted to turn the world upside down for her, but he couldn't. He wanted to soothe her pain, but he couldn't do that, either.

"It's all right," she said, and patted his hand. "The morning sickness will pass. The baby will come. The world will go on. All I need is for you to still love me." Her eyes filled with tears, and her smile crumpled. "I just need for you to still be my brother no matter what."

Houston kicked back his chair and came around the table to catch her in his arms as she collapsed in a heap of exhausted sobs. "I'm such a jerk," he said over the sound of her crying.

"P-pregnant w-women are emo-motional," she stuttered through a curtain of tears.

"If you don't want to marry that SOB, you don't have to. And I'll fight anybody who tries to make you."

Rebecca lifted her head from his shoulder and almost smiled. "Thank you."

"But I would like to talk to him."

"No."

"Dammit, Becky!"

"It's my baby, and it's my life," she said through gritted teeth.

He recognized the dangerous flash in her dark eyes and knew it was no use to argue. Gentle Rebecca could be a tigress when she was pushed too far. He held up his hands, indicating surrender. "Sorry. My big-brother impulses get out of control sometimes."

Always quick to forgive, Rebecca grinned. "And it can be a real pain, too."

Three rapid chimes of the doorbell interrupted Houston's rebuttal and brought him around to face the living room. "Who the hell could that be this time of morning?"

"Jessy. She's taking me to the doctor this morning. She's become a real mother hen since she found out." Rebecca patted her still flat stomach. "She's worried because I haven't been sleeping well."

Houston pointed to her chair. "Stay there. I'll get the door." Feeling as though it was all a nightmare and he'd be waking up any minute, he headed for the front door as another chorus of chimes rippled through the apartment. "Just a minute, dammit!" he shouted.

Three long strides later, he jerked the door open and faced Jessica, as different from her twin as dawn was from dusk.

One look at Houston and the smile on Jessy's face disappeared. Her hazel eyes huge with alarm, she clutched his forearm. "What's the matter? Is she all right?"

"She's fine." He drew her inside and closed the door. "Calm down."

"Did she sleep last night?"

"Not very well, I think." He looked at her and shook his head in wonderment. Fiery, flirty, head-strong Jessica was the one he had always worried about. She was the one who had always leaped without looking, who had grabbed at life with both hands, while Rebecca had been the cautious, patient one who had unerringly steered a safe course.

"I know I shouldn't," Jessy said with a sigh while she nervously raked her fingers through her tawny hair, "but I just can't help worrying about her. She's so delicate."

"Jessy." Houston frowned, uncertain if he should go on. Rebecca had clearly told him to stay out of it, but Jessy lived in Austin, too, only blocks from Rebecca. And while they were very different people, they must have shared some of the same friends. Maybe... He took a deep breath and looked hard into her amber and green eyes. "Jessica."

She gave him the same look of stubborn resistance that Rebecca had given him only minutes earlier. "Are you going to ask me about the father?"

"Do you know who he is?"

"What did Rebecca tell you?"

"You do know who he is."

She shook her head stubbornly. "If Rebecca hasn't told you, I'm not going to tell you."

"I just want to talk to him," Houston coaxed. "For the baby's sake, someone has to try to work this out."

The resolve in her eyes wavered, and Jessy lowered her gaze to the floor. When she finally looked into his eyes, it was with sorrow.

"If it would do any good, Houston, I'd tell you everything I know. But it wouldn't do any good, and it would just hurt Rebecca." She touched his arm and silently begged for his understanding. "Maybe someday, when the wound isn't so fresh, she'll be able to tell you herself."

Eight years older than his sisters, Houston had rocked them to sleep as infants, guided their first steps as toddlers and watched over them through the treacherous years of adolescence. And he had never loved them more or been prouder of them than he was at this moment.

"You're right," he said, taking her hand in his. "I won't worry about it anymore."

They were grown women now. They had their own lives to live and their own mistakes to make. He had a life of his own to get on with, and the best part of his life was waiting for him in Savannah, if he could only get there.

Chapter Seven

High noon traffic on River Street was heavy. With Christmas only two weeks away, the bustle of shoppers more closely resembled the height of tourist season. Even the river seemed busier than usual.

Laura folded her empty lunch sack in a neat square and dropped it into a trash can, then continued to walk toward the end of the street and the little monument of the Waving Girl.

Bronze skirt fluttering eternally in the breeze, the young girl lifted her handkerchief in salute to the passing ships, waving to the lover who had gone to sea one day and never returned.

Laura couldn't help thinking that the statue kept its lonely vigil for all lovers everywhere who were apart, and she found herself drawn to it every time she strolled beside the river.

It had been a week since Houston's first phone call, and he had called almost every morning since. But he was no closer to returning, and as she waited for him, Laura was discovering a new kind of loneliness.

It walked next to her beside the river. It haunted her thoughts on rainy afternoons. It held her hand by day and wrapped its cold arms around her each night.

She missed Houston with an aching emptiness that grew worse each minute of every passing day. And the only thing that scared her more than the idea of loving him was the thought of losing him.

He was still the wrong man at the wrong time. And yet, on the mornings he called, she felt a happiness she had never known before. And the days he didn't call were the longest she had ever lived through.

They had been together so little. He had barely kissed her, and still Houston had become the sunshine, the singing birds and the joy that seemed to follow her through her day. Just the thought of him could make her smile, blush or laugh out loud, and as much as it pained her to admit it, she couldn't help thinking that she must be in love.

"Darling, wait till you see what I've bought!"

At the sound of her mother's voice, Laura pulled back from her thoughts with a start and hastily coughed to camouflage the deep sigh she had just released.

They sat down together, and Julia set her packages at her feet and leaned closer. "Was that a sigh I just heard?"

For a woman who talked almost exclusively in exclamation marks, her mother could do an amazing job of reading other people's minds. "Yes," Laura answered, knowing it was hopeless to deny it.

"Want to talk about it?"

Laura was about to decline when she realized that she did want to talk about it, that she had wanted to talk about it since she had called her mother on Thanksgiving Day.

"I've met a man," she said simply.

Julia smiled a warm, gracious, dazzling smile that was like an extension of her personality. "That's wonderful."

"Not so wonderful," Laura said glumly.

"Oh." Instantly sympathetic, Julia touched her daughter's hand. "Why not?"

"He's a friend of Max's. A polo buddy."

"Mmm," Julia said with understanding. "He's older."

Laura shook her head. "No. He's young."

"Oh," Julia said, a little confused but still hopeful. "Is he nice?"

"Very." Laura couldn't help smiling as she thought of just how nice he was.

"Handsome?"

"Very," she said again, her smile growing wider and her thoughts turning to blue eyes and curly brown hair.

"And he returns your interest?"

Laura's smile evaporated in a sigh. "I think so." Uncertainty crept into her voice. "I'm pretty sure he does. I . . . I haven't really seen him in weeks. He's out of town right now."

"He isn't, by any chance, the absent contractor on your renovation, is he? The much-talked-about-and-never-seen Houston?"

Laura looked at her in amazement. Then she threw back her head and laughed.

"I thought so," Julia said. "You sort of glowed every time his name was mentioned."

Laura's laughter died in a gasp, and she lowered her head to frown at her mother. "I didn't."

"You did, dear," Julia insisted, nodding. "I'm pretty sure that nice Mr. Morgan has noticed it, too. But that's fine, sweetheart. There's nothing wrong with love." She smiled her sparkling smile again. "It makes people happy."

Laura found her mother's enthusiasm infectious but unrealistic. Resisting the temptation to agree with the sentiment, she argued, "Love makes people a lot of things. And not all of them are so wonderful."

"Oh, my." Julia's smile turned to a worried frown. "We're coming to the part about Max and polo and unhappy marriages, aren't we?"

"Well, wouldn't I be foolish not to think about it?" She stared at the river. It looked very blue and quiet and just a little lonely.

"Think about it, yes," her mother urged. "But don't let it make the decision for you, honey."

Laura's heart longed to agree, but her defenses were too long established to give in so easily. "How can you say that after what you've been through?" she demanded.

Julia put her hand over Laura's and looked deep into her eyes. "I have two wonderful daughters. And even if he is impossible to live with, I still love your father very much. I wouldn't trade my life for any-thing."

"Even after last night?" Laura could still visualize the fury in her father's eyes when her mother had walked into the house.

Julia's gaze turned away, and her whole body seemed to sag. "That was an ordeal, wasn't it?" she said with a sigh.

"I can't remember when I've seen him that angry."

Max had threatened and raged and fumed and blustered and finally had gone to the guest lodge to spend the night, and Laura, Julia and Etta had breathed a sigh of relief when he was gone.

Her eyes glazing over, Julia asked with a soft smile, "He is handsome, though, isn't he? After so many years I hadn't really expected him to still be so hand-some. And, you know, a funny thing happened."

Her mother turned to her, and Laura could see the years drop away. The woman next to her looked like a young woman in love and uncertain about what to do next.

"No matter what he did or said, I couldn't feel any anger," Julia continued with that same soft, thought-ful smile. "I could see his pain so clearly. I just wanted to hold him and tell him he didn't have to be afraid." She laughed. "Isn't that silly? He'd have had a stroke if I'd done it."

Resisting the urge to groan, Laura said, "It's going to be a long two weeks until Christmas."

"Don't let him fool you. He's happier to have us here than he lets on."

"Do you think so?" Laura could hear the eagerness in her voice, and it made her want to kick herself.

"I'm positive," Julia answered with determination. "He never wanted us to leave in the first place, but it took me a lot of years to realize it. And by the time I did, I didn't know how to undo what I'd done. Maybe this will be the right time. For all of us." Smiling, she patted Laura's hand. "So, when do I get to meet this young man of yours?"

Laura almost sighed again, but caught herself. It seemed the more hopeless she felt about Max, the more confused her feelings were about Houston. She missed him. She needed him. She wanted him. And she had never wanted to do any of those things.

"He should be back any day now," she said, trying not to let her dejection show. "Or a month from now. I'm really not sure, but by the first of the year Joe will have gone as far as he can go without Houston."

"You're pretty serious about him, aren't you? Have you, uh... how can I... um...?"

This time she did sigh. Knowing her mother well enough to read her mind, Laura interrupted her. "We haven't slept together, if that's what you're wanting to know."

"Ah," Julia said with a satisfied smile. "Excuse the motherly sigh of relief. It's instinctive. Now tell me why you haven't, since you're obviously crazy about him."

"Mother!" she cried indignantly. Beyond a brief birds-and-bees discussion when Laura was young, she and her mother had barely talked about sex, and this wasn't the day Laura wanted to begin.

"Sweetheart," Julia said gently, "Lorene was in love with someone new every other day, and I worried myself sick that she was going to do something foolish. So she and I talked a lot. But this is the first time I've seen you really serious about anyone. You and I still have a lot of ground to cover."

"I know about birth control," Laura said nervously.

Julia laughed. "I wasn't that negligent a mother. Now, how old is he?"

"Early thirties, I think." The more Julia asked, the more nervous Laura felt herself getting. Somehow, talking to her mother about Houston made everything she was feeling for him that much stronger.

"Has he ever been married?" Julia continued.

For a second, Laura didn't know how to answer. She really didn't know. There was a lot about Houston she didn't know and had never thought about. "I don't think so," she said slowly.

"Any children?"

"Mother!" Enough was enough. There were some things she hadn't thought about and didn't want to think about.

"Well, it happens," Julia said, as unflappable as ever. "I assume he doesn't live here?"

Giving in, Laura decided she might as well tell her mother everything she knew, which wasn't very much. "He's from Dallas," she said. "He's got a couple of brothers and sisters. He's from a ranching family. He's in business with his older brother. Seems close to his family and likes dangerous sports. Football, rodeo, polo. Anything where he can get his neck broken."

"And you think you're falling in love with him, and it scares you to death." Julia paused and grew thoughtful. "And yet, you hired him as your contractor, where you would have to be around him day after day for months."

"I thought I could handle it. I didn't think I'd miss him so much when he wasn't around. I didn't know how easy it would be to start depending on him. Or how much time I'd spend thinking about him."

"And how does he feel?"

"Damned if I know," Laura said with a shrug. At this point she was too exhausted to think about it, much less talk about it.

Julia shook her head and smiled, not buying the answer. "You must have some idea."

Laura let her breath out with a long sigh and caught herself just before she put her head in her hands. "I think he cares," she said reluctantly. "I think the only thing that's holding us back is me."

"And why is that?" Julia asked. She was a gentle but determined interrogator.

Laura turned to her mother and faced her fears head on. "I'm just plain scared, I guess. About almost everything. There are so many different things that can go wrong when you fall in love."

"Well, yes, but there are so many different things that can go right, too."

Laura shook her head, blocking out her mother's argument. "All I know is, the thought of putting myself at the mercy of love scares me to death," she said with feeling. "There are too many ways to be hurt."

"Ouch," Julia answered in a softly wounded voice.

"I'm sorry." Laura looked at her with pained eyes. She hadn't meant to hurt her mother, but she didn't know any other way to say what she felt.

"No, sweetheart, I'm sorry." Julia squeezed her hand. "I'm sorry that what happened between your father and me left such scars on our children. I'm sorry that for years I had to watch while Lorene ran desperately after love and you ran desperately away from it, and I'm sorry there was nothing I could do to help you."

Julia cupped Laura's cheek in her palm and looked deep into her eyes. "But Lorene finally found the love she needed. So just promise me you'll give this a fair chance, Laura, please. Real love is always a little scary. But if Houston's the right man, it'll be worth it. Trust me."

"I'll try."

"That's all you have to do. Nature will take care of the rest."

Houston turned his back on the crackling fireplace and took a sip of the eggnog he held in his hand. The heat of the fire radiated against his legs while he slowly studied the assembled members of his family.

Across the room his mother, Cissy, sat at the piano. Gathered around her were Rebecca, who hadn't wanted to come to the annual Christmas Eve gathering, Jessica, who had spent the evening protectively glued to her sister's side, and Susan, his sister-in-law, who had aligned herself with Houston as a peacemaker for the holiday.

Playing checkers in the corner were Hank Carder, the family patriarch, and Alan, his youngest child, who was enjoying the unusual status of being totally innocent. In another corner, within guarding distance of the Christmas tree, were Jack's children, J.J., aged seven, and Kelley, aged four.

"So," Jack said, joining Houston by the fireplace, "have you found out who the guy is yet?"

Houston shook his head. "Don't expect to. It's not something Rebecca wants to talk about right now, and I guess we're just going to have to respect her feelings."

Jack scowled. "How about Jessy? Won't she talk about it?"

"Remember when they were kids, and they'd decide to stick together on something? Well, that's what it's like now. And you're just wasting your breath if you try to argue with either one of them."

Jack laid a heavy hand on Houston's shoulder and said, "I'm disappointed. I was counting on you to get to the bottom of this. I may be the oldest, but you're the one who can talk to women. Susan's the only woman I've ever really been able to talk to, and I married her just as soon as I could get her to agree."

"There's a difference between talking and badgering, Jack, and I've taken this as far as I can. Rebecca doesn't want to talk about it, and there's nothing we can do except be there for her when she needs us."

"Damn." Jack took a sip of his drink and thought for a few seconds. "Well, what's she going to do? What does she need? What can I do to help?"

Houston shrugged his shoulders, understanding his brother's frustration but helpless to solve it. "I don't think even she knows yet. And all she really wants right now is for us to just shut up and show her that we still love her."

Jack hung his head in a rare gesture of defeat. "But I don't know what to say to her. You were always so much closer to them. And now, when it counts, I don't know how to reach out to her."

It was Houston's turn to lay a hand on Jack's shoulder. "It'll happen," he said quietly. "There'll come a time when it'll just happen naturally. Don't worry about it. She'll know."

Jack cocked his head and grinned a little sheepishly. "You know, you've grown up pretty good. I'm even a little ashamed of all the times I used to hassle you. I think I was always a little jealous because women just seemed to lean on you so naturally and tell you all their troubles."

A little uncomfortable with Jack's unexpected confession, Houston looked at him in bewilderment. "But, Jack, you were the one with women hanging off both arms until Susan came along. I was just friends with most of the women I knew. You were...well, you were a lot more than that."

Jack laughed. "Okay, I admit it. I wasn't hurting for company. But you could have made out like a bandit if you hadn't been so busy wiping their tears and putting bandages on their hurts."

"Hold on, now, I wasn't exactly an angel," Houston said, growing indignant. "I just always thought there was time for a little friendship before the sex."

Jack shook his head sadly. "Women were fighting to get next to you, and you never even knew it. Half the women I went out with were ones who'd given up on you."

"Cut it out now, Jack." He could hear the tone of teasing that had crept into his brother's voice.

"Scout's honor. You could have been a real animal if you weren't such a nice guy."

They both laughed at that, and Houston glanced over and saw that the sing-along around the piano had broken up. Susan had joined her children. Rebecca and Jessy were watching the game of checkers, and Cissy was headed toward her two sons in front of the fireplace.

"And what are you two whispering about?" she asked when she reached them. "If you were discussing your sister, you could have at least waited until I joined you."

Houston put his arms around his mother's shoulders and kissed the top of her head. "We finished that topic a long time ago. We'd moved on to women and sex."

She shrugged out of his restraining grasp and slapped his arm playfully. "Houston, Jack's a married man. You shouldn't be talking to him about things like that."

They all laughed, and Cissy slipped her arms through both of theirs. "There is something I'd like to talk to you about," she said quietly. "How much longer before you go back to Savannah, Houston?"

He glanced at Jack for confirmation. "About a week?"

Jack nodded.

"Personally, I'd like to be there for New Year's Eve," Houston told them both for the first time. "Why?"

"Well." His mother took a deep breath. "I guess it's understandable that Rebecca wouldn't want to go back to teaching school next semester. After all, she'll be showing in a couple of months and— Well, anyway, it leaves her at sort of loose ends. And it's my opinion that it wouldn't hurt her to travel a little."

Jack's puzzled gaze met Houston's over the top of their mother's head. "You mean like a cruise or something?" Jack asked her.

"More like going to Savannah with Houston," she said slowly. "If he thinks there would be a place for her." She looked directly at her second son. "I think it would do her good to keep busy if you could find something for her to do."

"Uh..." Houston said, stalling. He loved his sisters. He had cherished and protected them his whole life. But for the first time in his life he was truly and deeply in love, and he couldn't let anything or anyone come before Laura. Not right now.

"I could put her to work," Jack said helpfully. "That would get her out of Austin and give her something to do with herself."

His mother shook her head. "Dallas isn't far enough away. And as much as we all love her, this is still very hard for your father to accept. I think once he has a grandchild to see and to hold, he'll be able to put it behind him. But right now he's holding in too much anger, and Rebecca's too fragile to deal with it."

Houston nodded and let out his breath in a long, slow sigh. "Sure. I'll take her. I'll find something for her to do."

His mother smiled and patted his hand. "I knew you would, dear. And who knows but what it might not be a benefit for everyone in the long run. Aren't Rebecca and this young woman you're so taken with about the same age? Maybe they'll get to be friends and Rebecca can put in a good word for you.''

With that and another smile, she turned and made her way across the room to Susan and her grandchildren.

''Maybe you can stash her in a hotel room New Year's Eve,'' Jack suggested when their mother was out of earshot.

''I don't even want to think about it,'' Houston answered.

''Maybe Becky won't want to go.''

''I'm afraid Mom's right. It's about the only solution that makes sense.''

''I hope she's right about the rest of it. I really want this to work out for you, Houston. You deserve the best, and I'm not just saying that because I'm your brother. If this Laura has a brain in her head, she won't let you get away.''

''Well,'' Hank Carder announced, rising from the checker table, ''now that I've taught my youngest some manners, is everybody about ready to eat?''

Amid a chorus of assent, everyone began to drift toward the dining room.

Rebecca fell into step next to Houston. ''Eat, open gifts and go home. Right?'' she said under her breath.

''You got it. Is Jessy in agreement?''

''She's in charge of hustling things along as discreetly as possible.''

''Excellent assignment. You have definite leadership potential.''

''Thank you, kind sir.''

"How are you holding up?"

She sighed. "Okay."

"That doesn't sound okay."

"It's just that Mom is trying so hard, and Dad..." She sighed again, sounding dejected. "Well, he just doesn't know what to say. I broke all the rules."

"In this family, when you get serious, you get married," Houston quoted.

"You got it. Even Jack, after all the wild oats he sowed, still married the first girl he ever really loved."

"A legend in his own time," Houston said, thinking of the reputation his older brother once had and would have loved to pass on to Houston.

"And you," Rebecca said, squeezing his arm affectionately, "after dozens of infatuations and countless damsel-in-distress rescues, you go away for one week and come back pricing engagement rings."

Houston felt himself wince and glow at the same time. One more week and he'd be with Laura, and the thought filled him with such happiness it was almost embarrassing.

"Look at you," Rebecca said, shaking her head. "I used to think Jack had it bad for Susan, but I think you've set a new family record."

He shrugged. "Just an old-fashioned boy, I guess."

"From an old-fashioned family. And I'm just another damsel in distress."

Houston smoothed her dark hair away from her pale face. "You'll never be just another anything, Rebecca. You're one of a kind and very special. And I want you to always remember that."

She smiled at him. "Because my big brother says so."

"That's right."

Still wrapped in the cobwebs of sleep, Laura rolled toward the phone and had it in her hand by the end of the first ring. Squinting to make out the time on her bedside clock, she mumbled a groggy hello.

"I woke you, didn't I?" Houston said apologetically.

The luminous green numbers next to the phone read 12:45 a.m. "Only partially." Laura muffled a yawn and pulled the phone into the pillows with her. "If my eyes don't open, it doesn't really count."

"This is really rude of me. I should call back tomorrow."

"No, this is fine." She pulled another pillow under her head and tried to sound awake. She didn't want him to hang up. "This is nice, actually. Merry Christmas."

"Are you sure you don't mind? I don't know what I was thinking of to call so late."

"What are you doing up?" she asked, holding the phone closer and lowering her voice to a cozy midnight pitch. "Trying to catch Santa Claus in the act?"

"I've been out to the ranch. Santa Claus comes on Christmas Eve in my family."

"He bring you anything nice?"

"I'm still waiting to see. Do you have plans for New Year's Eve?"

The steady beat of her heart kicked into a heavy thud. "No," she said, wide awake and trying not to sound overly excited. "Not a thing."

"Well, the best Christmas present I could have would be to see the New Year in with you. It would make me a happy man if you'd be my date for the night."

"Oh, Houston." Laura cradled the phone in both hands and sat up against the high walnut headboard.

"Is that 'oh, Houston, yes' or 'oh, Houston, no'?"

"Oh, Houston, yes. I'd love to. I'd really love to."

"I probably won't be there until that day, but don't worry, I'll take care of the arrangements from here. And I found a present for you that I think you'll like. Sort of a combination Christmas present and house-warming gift."

She smiled, very pleased. She loved presents. Any presents. "What is it?"

"It's a surprise, and I'll give it to you at midnight."

"Oh, Houston," Laura coaxed. "Can't you just give me a hint? Is it big or small? Would it rattle if I shook it?"

He laughed. "It's big, and it might rattle. It depends on how hard you shook it. But that's all the hints you get or it won't be a surprise."

"Now, Houston, that's not fair. You call me in the middle of the night, wake me up, then torture me with secrets so I'll never get to sleep."

"Well, I guess it's best you found out the truth about me before things got too serious between us," he joked.

"I'm not sure it was soon enough," Laura answered in an undertone that was almost inaudible.

There was a pause, and then, his "What?" sounded more like a breathless wheeze than a question.

Moonlight, and starlight, and the black magic of night caught her in their seductive rays. It was madness, but she wanted to tell him.

"I've missed you more than I thought I would. I've missed you more than I thought I could," she said quietly.

"Laura, you don't know how much I've wanted to hear you say that." His words came in an elated rush. "I've had to hold my breath to keep from telling you how much I've missed you, how much I think about you, how much you mean to me." He slowed down. "I didn't want to scare you off by saying too much."

"I didn't get you anything for Christmas," Laura said, a little sad that she hadn't. She had found a hundred things that she'd wanted to get for him, but she'd been afraid to.

"Yes, you did," he said. "You told me that you missed me, and that's the best present I could have had."

"I really should get you something more," she went on. "If only I knew what you'd gotten me, I'd have a better idea of what to get for you."

Houston laughed. "You're relentless, aren't you? I'll bet you're one of those people who messes with every present under the Christmas tree."

"No, I don't," she said firmly. "Just the ones with my name on them. Look, some people can stand secrets and some people can't. I can't. So, is it something I'll have to water?"

Houston laughed harder. "Okay, okay. I'll send it on ahead. But I won't tell you what it is. You'll just have to see for yourself."

"Oh, Houston, thank you." She snuggled into her pillows, wondering what it could be, but content to wait a few days for it to arrive.

"How's your apartment? Joe says it's about ready."

"It's going to be so cozy. Right now the only piece of furniture I have for it is a big square coffee table I found at a farm auction last week. I'm going to put a rug down, and put some pillows around, and once I get a bed, it'll be enough for a while." The tone of her voice deepened, growing more intimate. "The view is wonderful, and the river in the moonlight is breathtaking."

"Maybe you can show me when I get back."

"New Year's Eve might be a nice time." She never looked out those windows without imagining him by her side.

"It's a date."

Laura drew in a huge, yawning breath and exhaled. "That sounds terrific."

"I beg your pardon?"

"That sounds terrific," she repeated as she stretched.

"And you sound tired."

"Relaxed. And happy." She yawned again. "This has been a wonderful Christmas already."

"For me, too. I think I'm about ready to turn in myself. See you next week?"

"I'll be waiting." Snuggling deeper into the bed, she said, "Sweet dreams."

"You, too," he answered softly.

Over the sound of the dial tone after he had hung up, Laura whispered, "I love you," and set the receiver on the cradle.

Chapter Eight

Houston nervously glanced at his watch and grimaced.

"I'm sure she'll understand," Rebecca said softly.

He adjusted his grip on the steering wheel and edged the speedometer up a few more miles per hour.

"It's always hard to get away when there are so many people to say goodbye to," Rebecca continued in the same soothing tone. Then she chuckled. "Especially when they insist on throwing you a farewell party."

"I think the party was more for you," Houston said, slowing down for a curve and sending gravel flying on the shoulder of the road.

Rebecca calmly braced one hand against the dashboard and shook her head. "They're really not sure when they're going to see you again. And you were always their favorite.''

Shocked, Houston took his eyes from the road and stared at her. ''No, I wasn't.''

''Yes, you were,'' she insisted, laughing. ''The rest of us were sort of relieved, because we could tell they put a lot more pressure on you. Being the favorite isn't easy, and we were all very grateful to you for carrying the burden.''

Houston frowned at the road. ''I always thought you were the favorite.''

Rebecca sighed heavily. ''Well, next to you, I was. And look how I turned out. There were times when I used to envy Jack and Alan and Jessy. They were the ones who really had the freedom.''

Houston looked at her thoughtfully. ''Becky,'' he said quietly, ''you didn't do this on purpose, by any chance, did you?''

''This?'' Rebecca asked, patting her stomach. She laughed and shook her head. ''No. Not consciously, anyway. But it was a pretty Freudian accident, wasn't it? So who knows?''

He eased up on the accelerator. The hour didn't seem quite so late anymore, and they only had a little farther to go. He could give her some time. ''I never knew you were unhappy.''

She rested her head against the back of the seat and stared at the night through the open sunroof. ''Everybody's unhappy at one time or another, Houston. Haven't you been?''

''Sure, I guess. I know I've been lonely.''

''Lonely. Yeah, I've been that, too. Living up to other people's expectations is never easy, and I think that's something I've spent too much of my life trying to do. Now that I seem to have blown it in a big way, I thought maybe this would be a good time to evaluate what I really want to do with my life.''

Her words hit home, and Houston realized he had been doing the same thing recently. He had always been a rancher at heart, and the chance to buy the Polo Station had been a dream come true. But the dream wouldn't be perfect until he had someone to share it with.

He wasn't a solitary man. Happiness to him had always been family. He wanted a marriage like his parents had, like his brother had. He wanted a woman by his side to love and grow old with. He wanted the woman who'd touched his heart and made it her own the day he'd met her. He wanted Laura.

"Poor guy." Rebecca's soft voice called him from his thoughts. Her strong fingers massaged the tense muscles in his neck. "You're going to be so tired when we get there."

"Ooh," Houston crooned, luxuriating in the warm, soothing feel of her massage. A numbing relaxation spread across his shoulders and down his arms. "Whoa, Florence Nightingale, you better cut it out before I fall asleep and we end up in a ditch."

Laughing, Rebecca hastily withdrew. "Speaking of ditches, what are you and Laura doing tonight?"

"Well, I called Joe and had him set up some champagne on ice, along with some snacks, and I thought maybe some dinner and dancing before that, but . . ." He checked his watch. It was after nine.

"You're running out of time, aren't you?"

"It's getting pretty close."

Rebecca consoled him with, "At least you'll be with her at midnight, even if the rest of the evening hasn't been what you'd planned."

Houston glanced toward her, a worried frown creasing his brow. "Are you sure you'll—"

"I'll be fine," she interrupted. "After the past two days, all I want to do tonight is sleep. A glass of warm milk and a soft bed are all the celebration I want."

"Well, if you're sure, because—"

She laughed. "It's your night, Houston. Take it and run."

"Thank you very much. I think I will," he said, laughing with her. He hated to drag his little sister halfway across the country and then abandon her among strangers on one of the most significant nights of the year. But he hated even more to have anything interfere with his reunion with Laura.

Ahead was a towering wall of trees, and the road seemed to disappear into the middle of it. Transported back in time, Houston grinned and checked his watch again. Just a few more minutes and he would be reunited with the cutest little drowned rat he'd ever rescued.

He slowed down for the sharp curve and looked toward the ditch. The skid marks were gone. A cold chill ran up his back at the thought of what might have happened.

"That's the curve, isn't it?" Rebecca asked.

"Yeah," he answered.

"At least it turned out all right," she said quietly. "Was that the night you fell in love?"

The curve behind him, the stable ahead and the end of the long trip in sight, Houston allowed himself to relax and savor the good parts of the memory. "It was the beginning of it."

"You know, I'm really glad you've found Laura. I was beginning to wonder if it was ever going to happen."

"If what was going to happen?"

"If you were ever going to fall in love. I mean, you've always had a lot of girlfriends, but that's all they were. Just friends." She laughed. "It used to drive Jack crazy the way girls would flock around you and make up problems to get your attention."

Houston turned to look at her and asked distinctly, "Make up problems?"

Rebecca shrugged. "You were known far and wide as a soft touch. So if they couldn't get your attention one way, they just appealed to your sympathy and hoped for the best."

"You're kidding me."

"Nope." She laughed again. "You left some very frustrated females in your wake."

"That's scary. You knew this, and you never told me?"

"I never needed to. I never saw you give the phonies more than a sympathetic ear and a pat on the rump before you sent them on their way. I finally decided you must have some sort of built-in radar. And I didn't want to see you change. I liked you the way you were."

He took her hand and squeezed it. "I feel the same way about you, little sister. If you ever need anything, promise me you'll let me know? I don't want you to be unhappy, or lonely, or to do without anything while I'm around. Okay?"

"If it'll make you happy, I'll let you spoil me rotten." She looked at the road ahead, and her eyes grew round with surprise. "Wow."

Following her gaze, Houston saw the main house lit up as he had never seen it before. Christmas lights were strung along the roof and around the front door and windows. The trees in front were festooned with strings of starry white lights. The dignified old mansion looked younger and gayer than he had ever seen it.

"This is the place you're buying?" Rebecca asked incredulously. "It's a mansion, Houston. Just how many kids are you planning to have, anyway?"

Reality came back with a rush. The secrets, the strife and the hidden tensions that pervaded the atmosphere of the house came into crystalline focus, and Houston asked warily, "Did I mention that Laura doesn't know anything about the sale?"

"No," Rebecca answered slowly, "I don't think you did. When are you planning to tell her?"

"When the deal's final. When we're engaged. I'm not really too sure about that part yet."

"You don't think she'll feel deceived?"

Houston followed the curved drive and came to a stop just past the front door. "Oh, I'm sure she will," he said with a sigh. "Also, Max doesn't know anything about the place she's fixing up on River Street."

"Oh, Houston," Rebecca said warily.

"I know."

"And you want to marry this woman? I think the first thing you need to do is to get everything out in the open," she said firmly.

"I'd love to. But they aren't my secrets to reveal."

"But you're the one who's going to get caught in the middle," she insisted.

"You're absolutely right." He glanced toward the house and saw the front door open. "But we're going to have to finish this another day. We've been discovered."

His heart beat faster, partly from excitement and partly from dread. He hadn't wanted to think about how volatile his situation was, but Rebecca's reaction had forced him to face it. He'd kept the truth from Laura for as long as he dared.

When the door opened wider and Etta stepped out onto the front terrace, he was almost relieved. The month he had been gone seemed more like a year, and now that Laura was only a few yards away, he needed a few more minutes to collect his thoughts.

"Oh, gosh," Rebecca said nervously. "I almost wish I'd stayed home." She reached into the back seat and began to gather up her things—a sweater coat, purse and canvas overnight bag.

"Are you getting shy on me?" Houston joked as he took the bag from her.

"I think panic-stricken is a closer description."

He came around and opened her car door. "Is there anything in the trunk that you need?"

"Later. I don't want to look like I'm moving in."

He held her hand reassuringly, and they started toward the house. "Try to relax. Everyone's friendly, basically. Max is a little gruff sometimes, but after Dad, that shouldn't be anything new."

Etta came down the steps to greet them. She took Rebecca's hand warmly.

"Rebecca, this is Etta," Houston said as they crossed the terrace. "She runs the house and cooks the best food you've ever tasted. And by the time you leave here, she'll probably be one of the best friends you've ever had."

Etta blushed and patted Rebecca's arm. "Now don't you pay any attention to him, dear. He just says things like that so he'll get double portions at mealtime."

"Does it work?" Rebecca asked, laughing.

"Indeed it does," Etta said, smiling.

They walked through the foyer and into the living room together, a happy, relaxed trio. "Mr. Houston Carder and his sister Rebecca have arrived," Etta announced formally. Then she quickly unstiffened and said, "Houston, you haven't met Mrs. Warner, have you?"

Houston had already scanned the room for Laura and was disappointed not to find her. But to meet Max's long-absent wife was almost momentous enough to take the edge off of his dejection.

"Mrs. Warner," he said, taking the hand of the lovely dark-haired woman who rose to meet him.

"Call me Julia," she said in the honeyed voice of a lifelong Southern belle. Her dark eyes flashed meaningfully, and she continued in that light, lilting drawl, "I'm afraid you've missed Laura. Rebecca, dear." She took Rebecca's hand and led her to the sofa. "Do sit down. I know you must be tired."

Then, with an airy wave of her hand, Julia turned and said, "Where was it Laura was going, Max dear? Oh, yes, I remember." When she turned back to Houston, her eyes were directed only at him. "She was going to a little dinner party at a friend's, and then she was going down to River Street to meet another friend from out of town. I just mentioned this because you being young people yourselves—'' she smiled warmly at Rebecca then turned to Houston ''—and this being New Year's Eve and all, you might want to get out and do something festive instead of just sitting around this old place with Max and me.''

Houston smiled, grateful to Julia for the message. Laura was waiting for him at her place. He looked at his watch and forced down rising anxiety. He didn't know how long she had been waiting, and Julia had already told him all she could without arousing Max's suspicion.

''Well, Rebecca's already told me she'd rather stay home and get some rest.'' Houston sat on the arm of the couch next to Rebecca. ''But I think I would like to drive on into Savannah to take a look around. It always gives me a sense of homecoming to take a stroll down River Street whenever I've been away.''

''I know how you feel,'' Julia said, returning to the sofa opposite them. Her duty done, she was more relaxed, her words a little slower, her tone a little softer. ''I always take a long drive through the historic district whenever I come back, just so I know I'm really here. I'm afraid I can't remember the name of that place where Laura said she'd be. Can you, Max?''

Max's wheelchair was next to her at the end of the sofa, but he had sat mute since Etta had ushered Houston and Rebecca into the room. Now Max scowled first at Houston, then at Julia. ''All she said to me was goodbye,'' he grumbled.

"Oh." Julia looked at him with round, blank eyes, and then looked at Houston and smiled serenely. "Oh, well."

Houston smothered a laugh as he stood and reached for Max's hand. "Well, you'll probably be in bed by the time I get back tonight, Max, so I guess I'll see you in the morning."

Max gripped his hand without much enthusiasm. "Yeah."

"Maybe we can watch a little football tomorrow," Houston coaxed. "Knock back a few brews." He realized that Max must be miserable, surrounded by so many women, and probably deeply resented Houston's desertion so soon after his arrival, but it couldn't be helped.

Backing away, Houston said, "I'm trusting you to get Rebecca settled in, Julia."

Julia answered, "Like she's my own daughter."

At the same time Rebecca replied, "I'm a grown woman, Houston. I can climb stairs, and turn down beds and change clothes and everything all by myself."

Houston reached over the back of the couch and kissed Rebecca's frown away. "I have this problem with being overly protective," he told Julia with a grin. "But I'm working on it."

"Not hard enough," Rebecca said, folding her arms in good-natured disgust.

"You all have a really nice New Year's Eve." Houston held up a hand in goodbye as he left the room. "I'm leaving now before I get into any more trouble."

"Drive carefully," Julia called.

Just before he was out of sight, Rebecca turned and blew him a kiss. "Have a good time," she said with a mischievous smile.

"I certainly intend to." With a final smile, he was on his way. Into the night, into the new year, into the arms of the woman he loved. He couldn't remember when he had felt so good.

Laura sipped from the glass of white wine she held in her hand. She glanced longingly at the unopened bottle of champagne that sat in a bucket of melting ice on her kitchen counter, and she felt her spirits droop a little.

In the refrigerator was a tray of cold cuts, another of vegetables and half a dozen different dips and cheeses. On the counter, crackers and tiny loaves of homemade bread stayed fresh under plastic, and nuts waited to be served in small silver bowls.

Beside the chilled champagne was a basket filled with even more cheeses, crackers, tins of nuts, a canned ham, fruit, candies, even candied fruit. She hadn't taken the cellophane off yet, but the variety visible inside the basket was boggling.

Laura had brought the wine and more than enough food for two only to find a bucket of iced champagne and the wrapped basket of food waiting in the kitchen beside a huge vase of fresh flowers. It seemed that Houston had managed to have everything but himself delivered on time.

Strolling to the tall windows, she checked her watch by the light of the moon. It was almost eleven. Below, the street was alive with the sounds of laughter, snatches of music and the tooting of party horns.

Along the river couples walked arm in arm, bathed in the soft glow of the streetlights.

With sighs that grew heavier with each passing minute, Laura turned to gaze at the room that would be her home. At one end were the entryway and bathroom, at the other end was the kitchen. The wall that stretched between them was solid brick, once a deep red, now faded to a rose pink by the years.

The only piece of furniture along the wall was an antique brass and porcelain canopy bed that had been Houston's present along with a delicate crocheted canopy.

A few days after his Christmas telephone call, she had walked into the apartment to find the bed in place, wrapped with a huge ribbon and bow. Laura had immediately rearranged her plans for the day and gone to shop for the perfect sheet and comforter set, finding it in a floral cotton in shades of red and blue, with white eyelet ruffles and more matching pillows than she could ever use. But all together it was beautiful to behold, and every time she looked at the bed, she felt that the cavernous room could really be a home.

Her gaze continued to the far end of the apartment where the new U-shaped kitchen dominated. The tile counter that faced the room doubled as a breakfast bar, and at the open end of the kitchen there was still room for a large dining table. At the moment the space was occupied by a small round wicker table and two wicker armchairs that looked more as if they should be tucked into the corner of a bedroom. But they were all she had, and they would have to do.

The only other furniture were a few chests along the walls and a large, square coffee table in front of the three windows. She had bought some white flokati rugs and large throw pillows and scattered them around the coffee table. The overhead lighting was in the kitchen and bathroom and over the little wicker table.

In place of lamps that were yet to be purchased, candles flickered throughout the room. From wall sconces, candelabras and tiny votive cups, they released myriad sweet scents and cast a lovely wavering glow.

While she stood trying to decide what to do next, the knocker sounded at the door, and Laura jumped at the sudden sound in the silence. Her first impulse was to run to the door and throw it open, but she forced herself to walk.

It had to be Houston. There was no one else it could be, but the nearer she got to the door, the more she realized how terribly alone she was in the empty building and the slower her steps became.

At the door, she leaned near and asked, "Who is it?" in a voice that sounded far from confident.

On the other side, she heard Houston laugh. "Put away your baseball bat, it's me. Finally."

She took the chain off the door, turned the dead bolt and peeked around the door as she opened it. "I forgot to bring a baseball bat."

"I guess I'll have to get you one." He stepped across the threshold, then stopped just inside the open door to stare at her. "You've gotten prettier while I was gone," he said with a look that could have melted butter.

At the sudden trip-hammering of her heart, Laura lowered her gaze and self-consciously brushed aside the compliment. "It's the candlelight."

Houston caught her chin and tilted her face until her eyes met his. "I don't think so." He brushed the backs of his fingers against her temple. "I like your hair like that."

She had spent hours on it, rolling it, brushing it, taming it into full, smooth waves that flowed past her shoulders. It was a style she had copied from a magazine, a style that had seemed sultry and sophisticated at the same time, a way she had always wanted to look but had been afraid to try.

"Thank you." She could almost feel herself blushing.

He stepped back and held her hands out to her sides while he inspected her all the way down to her toes. "You look wonderful," he said when his gaze had made the return trip.

Laura gave in finally to the smile that was fighting to be free. Her dress was pale pink and strapless, with a heart-shaped bodice and a figure-molding torso. At the drop waist it flared into a full, frothy skirt that ended just above her knees. Her stockings were sheer, black and seamed, and her high-heeled evening sandals were the same soft pink as her dress. Taken all together, it was the most blatantly feminine outfit she could remember owning, and she would never have worn it if her mother hadn't pushed her every step of the way.

"I feel a little like a fairy princess," she confessed shyly. "I'm not really used to things like this."

"You should be." He lifted her hands to his lips and kissed each one with reverence. "I think you're the most beautiful thing I've ever seen." He turned her hands over and kissed the inside of each wrist, leaving the burning imprint of his lips on her skin. "You're much too beautiful to stay hidden away in here. You should be out where everyone can see you."

Vaguely Laura remembered her vow not to be swept away by her feelings, or Houston's charm, or the romance of the night. "But it's so late," she protested weakly, trying to remember why she had made the vow in the first place.

"We can take a walk along the river. It's not too late for that."

She thought of the couples she had watched from the window and how she had longed to be one of them. It was New Year's Eve. She had spent days getting ready, and Houston had traveled so far to be with her on this night. Casting her vow to the wind, she laughed and pulled him toward the door. "Let's go."

As they went down the staircase, he slipped his arm around her waist. "I'm sorry I was late."

"You can't control the airlines."

"I can't control my family, either. I drove."

Surprised, she turned her head and stared at him over her shoulder. "You drove? But you left your car here."

"Well, I brought my sister with me, and we drove her car so she'd have it here."

"Oh." A little puzzled, Laura wondered how much more she could ask before it would seem like prying. "Is this the sister who was staying with you? Did she ever decide what she's going to do?"

"She decided against marriage."

If Houston's tight-lipped responses were any indication, now was not the time to pursue that subject. Instead, Laura said, "Well, I guess you must be pretty tired, then, after such a long drive. When did you leave Dallas?"

Houston unlocked the door that led to the newly painted wrought-iron staircase and held it open for her.

"Well," he replied, slipping an arm around her waist as they started down the stairs to River Street, "we were supposed to leave yesterday morning, but my parents decided to give us a real send-off. They must have invited half the county over for a Texas-style barbecue in our honor, so it was evening before we could get away. I probably would have driven straight through, but with Rebecca along, I decided it wouldn't be wise."

They left the stairs, crossed the sidewalk and easily wound their way through the slow-moving parade of cars that cruised River Street. All around them party horns tooted, whistles trilled and clackers added to the racket. Sometimes muffled by distance, sometimes suddenly near, the sounds gave the night a special excitement.

Catching the festive spirit, Laura laughed and snuggled against Houston's side. Despite the time of year, the southern air was almost warm, but the breeze that blew from the river was damp and cold, and she was grateful for the protection of his arm.

"Here I was worrying about you," she said, only half teasing, "and you were late because of a party."

Stopping to gaze at the river, Houston slid her in front of him and crossed his arms over hers to keep her warm. "But I didn't enjoy myself at all."

She laughed again. "Well, in that case, I guess it's all right."

"I really didn't," he said softly, and laid his cheek against her hair. "In fact, I almost didn't stay for it."

Laura tilted her head and stared at him, her face only inches from his. "Really?"

"Really." He looked into her eyes, totally serious. "The only reason I stayed was that it was for Rebecca, too, and I didn't want to spoil it for her."

Happiness, delectably warm and fulfilling, bubbled inside her. For the past month, while Houston had been with his family and she had been impatiently awaiting his return, Laura had been so jealous she was ashamed of herself. To know that he had been willing to defy his family to be with her sooner moved her so deeply she almost cried.

"Houston." Her heart pounding in her throat, she turned in his arms and looked into his eyes.

"Oh, God, Laura." He released his words in a sigh as he gathered her to him. "I've missed you so."

"Oh, Houston." All the lonely days and nights came rushing toward her. She loved him, needed him, wanted him, and she never wanted to be without him again.

He kissed her then. Deep and hard and slow, and the night ended and began again in that kiss. When the kiss finally ended, she laid her head on his chest and tried to catch her breath.

"I think I love you," Houston said quietly.

Laura nodded and nestled against him contentedly. She knew he loved her. She'd always known he loved her, just as she'd always known she loved him. It was her stubbornness that hadn't let her admit it.

"In fact, I'm positive I love you," he said. "And I'm pretty sure you love me." He brushed his hand down her hair and cradled her head closer to his chest. "But it would mean a lot to me to hear you say it."

Laura took a deep breath and opened her mouth. But nothing came out. She'd said the words to two men in her lifetime—her father and her grandfather. She had always thought that the words "I love you" just sort of popped out when the time was right.

She tried again, and still the words wouldn't come. She could hear them in her mind, but they wouldn't go any farther. Finally she exhaled and stared at him.

"You're not ready, are you?" he asked softly.

The look on his face was one she'd seen before, the night he'd rescued her from the ditch, the night he hadn't wanted to sleep alone.

She hadn't been ready that night, either, and she'd had to watch him turn and walk away. She held her breath, waiting for him to walk away again and praying that this time he wouldn't.

"It's okay," Houston said gently. His thumb brushed away the tear that had formed at the corner of her eye. "They're only words. You don't have to say them until you're ready."

Rising on her tiptoes, she touched her lips to his. Tentatively at first, then with growing passion she told him in the only way she could. Her love, her desire, her longing poured out of her in a searing kiss that left them both shaken.

"Laura, Laura, baby," Houston whispered. "You don't have to prove anything to me." He smoothed his fingertips over her cheek. "I understand, honestly I do."

Frustrated with her confused emotions, Laura gave him a grin that was just a little lopsided. "I'm glad one of us does."

Laughing softly, he slipped his hand into hers. "Tonight's supposed to be a celebration. Come on." He began to walk with her along the river. "Fallen off any horses since I've been gone?"

Taking his lead, she answered lightly, "I haven't been riding. The contractor I hired has been out of town, and I've been too busy running errands he should be taking care of."

"The cad. Have you considered firing him and getting someone else?"

Feigning round-eyed shock, Laura said, "Oh, goodness, no. He's worth waiting for."

Abruptly he stopped and pulled her into his arms. "I'm glad you think so."

"I'm not sure thinking has much to do with it anymore. It seems to be more of an emotional response."

He brushed her lips with his. "Now I'm really glad."

Nothing seemed more natural than to melt into his arms while her pulse pounded from his kiss and her whole body came alive at his touch.

When they finally parted, Laura was still reeling from the intensity of her emotions. The night seemed suddenly as hot as high noon in August and was filled with a strange, rhythmic chanting. As her head cleared enough for her to distinguish the real from the imagined, Laura realized the people around them were counting.

"Houston." She caught his arm in excitement, feeling that the night had given them a special gift.

"I know." He held up his watch and slipped his arm around her so they both could see its face.

The crowd's countdown had gone from thirty to twenty, then into the teens. Houston pulled her closer and said, "Pucker up."

The countdown was at ten. Laura laughed and rose onto her tiptoes. "This is fun."

On the count of five, he lowered his head toward hers, very slowly, and at the count of one, his lips touched hers, and once again she was lost in a kiss that was like nothing she had ever known.

An old year was ending. A new one was beginning. And somehow she knew that the night, like the kiss, would be like nothing she had known.

Chapter Nine

Houston held her loosely around the waist and smiled at her. "Happy New Year, sweetheart."

Laura slid her arms around his neck and laughed. It was a terrific New Year's Eve. The kind she'd always dreamed of. "It's beautiful," she said, tilting her head to bestow a dazzling smile on the inky night sky. "And I'm very happy."

Houston leaned over and trailed light kisses across her exposed throat. "That makes two of us," he said, straightening. "Want to crash a party at one of these clubs?"

"Is that what you want to do?" She knew she'd enjoy anything they did so long as they were together, but a crowded club wasn't her first choice.

He shook his head and smiled. "I'd rather be alone with you."

"Well, I know a quiet little place where there's enough food for an army and a whole bottle of champagne that hasn't even been opened. I don't suppose you're hungry."

"I'm starved."

"Great. That champagne's been calling my name all evening, and I kept telling it that I had to wait for you."

Holding her close to his side, Houston led her along the river toward her building. "Sorry. If I'd known it was going to get fresh I'd never have left you alone with it."

"Who delivered that stuff, anyway? It startled me for a minute when I walked in and found it there."

"Joe. He took care of the bed, too."

She nodded. "Joe, naturally. Speaking of that bed—which I absolutely adore, by the way, and want to thank you very much for—but I'm just not sure it's really very proper."

"For a gentleman to give a lady a bed?" Houston asked. "I know, and I apologize for that, but it's awfully pretty, and it's exactly what you wanted, now, isn't it?"

"Well, yes."

"Because the minute I saw it, I remembered you saying how much you wanted a brass canopy bed for that apartment."

"Well, yes," she said again. "But it's so expensive, and so personal." Then she laughed, remembering the day she and her mother had walked in and found it. "You should have seen Mother's face. I thought for a minute she was going to make me take it apart and send it right back to you."

He lifted her hand and kissed it softly. "Maybe giving you a bed as a gift was in questionable taste, but the gesture was well intended. It was a gift I enjoyed giving and you enjoyed having, and if you're happy and I'm happy, I don't really care what anybody says about it. What do you think?"

Laura laughed and leaned closer to whisper, "I think I love it."

When they reached her apartment, Houston opened the door for her and guided her inside. They both looked automatically at the bed. Candlelight reflecting on the brass, white ruffles shining against dark florals, it looked comfortable and graceful and very much at home.

"I like what you've done with it," Houston said, closing the door.

"Thank you."

"In fact, as much as I didn't like the idea in the beginning, I think this is going to be a really nice place when you get through with it. It has a nice feel to it."

Laura grinned at him. "It's the candlelight," she teased, her earlier discomfort entirely gone.

Houston shook his head and slid his arms around her waist, pulling her close. "It's the woman behind the candles. It's Miss Laura Warner, with a style and a spirit and a beauty like none I've ever known. I don't know how I stayed away from you for a whole month."

"It was over a month," Laura gently reminded him, not forgetting a minute of her long, lonely wait.

"So it was. I'm glad you noticed."

His lips brushed hers, and a tickling, burning heat coiled inside her. She couldn't imagine ever loving anyone more. She couldn't imagine ever being happier with anyone.

"Ah, Laura." He whispered her name like a sigh and slid his hands through her hair to hold her face inches from his. "Feed me before I forget myself."

She gazed at him and felt a hot sensuality she had never felt before coursing through her veins. "Kiss me first," she demanded in a husky drawl that was just barely teasing. "Really kiss me."

"Oh, Laura," he moaned, and crushed her against him as his mouth covered hers.

Maybe it was the bed being so near. Or maybe it was the party still going on outside. Or maybe it was because it was so late at night, but she felt wild and daring and sexual for the first time in her life.

She was in love, and she was alone with a man whose touch made her think things and feel things she had never thought or felt before. A man whose kiss left her light-headed and weak-kneed, seeing visions of shooting stars and dreaming dreams of Rhett lifting Scarlett into his arms and sweeping up the staircase with her.

When the kiss was over, Laura couldn't have moved if she'd had to. Instead, she clung to Houston and felt his strong arms tighten around her while she struggled to regain her senses.

She had given up denying that she wanted him, and she knew he wanted her just as much. But she couldn't tell him how she felt any more than she could tell him how much she loved him. She didn't know what it would take to break loose the dam inside her, but she knew if any man could find the key, Houston would.

"I'll get the cheese if you'll open the champagne," she said in a voice that wasn't quite steady.

"Teamwork. I like that."

She smiled, feeling warmed inside by his words while they put their arms around each other's waists and walked the length of the room to the kitchen.

When he had opened the champagne, and they had arranged the trays and platters and bowls of food on the coffee table and piled pillows on a rug of woven sheep's hair, they sat, shoulder to shoulder, and sipped their champagne and dipped and crunched and nibbled and talked and laughed as the night wore on.

Finally Houston shoved himself away from the table and collapsed onto the pile of pillows behind him. He folded his arms under his head and stared at the ceiling. "I'm a happy man. A very full, very happy man." He stretched a hand out to Laura. "Join me?"

Setting down her champagne glass, she seated herself beside him, carefully arranging her full skirt. If he hadn't been watching her, she would have tugged the bodice a little higher. The longer she wore the dress, the smaller it seemed to be.

He took her hand in his and stroked her wrist with his thumb. "You could come a little closer."

She smiled, feeling shy once again. "But I might muss my lovely frock," she joked, and moved no nearer.

He pulled her hand to his lips and kissed it. "You're a never-ending challenge, Miss Warner."

She could feel the champagne buzzing through her head. She could feel the heat of his touch and his need igniting sparks inside her. The night was old and whispering to her of mysteries still to explore.

He turned her hand over and kissed the inside of her wrist. "I'm in no hurry, sweetheart." He shoved himself up on one elbow and brushed her cheek with his fingertips. "It's enough to be here with you. And if that's all you ever want, then that's all there'll ever be. And I'll just try to be happy with it."

Laura laughed softly, and said, "My sister, Lorene, always said to never trust a man who said he wasn't going to try anything. She said it was in a man's nature to try. And in a woman's nature to want him to."

"And what did you think?"

"I used to think she was wrong. I used to think I'd never feel that way."

"What do you think now?"

She laid her hand against his chest and felt the pounding of his heart. "I think I want you to try. I think I'd be very disappointed if you didn't."

"Thank God." Houston smiled softly and leaned toward her. His lips covered hers in a warm, gentle kiss, and his arms gathered her to him.

"I don't know a smooth way to say this," he whispered, breaking the kiss, "so I'm just going to say it."

Her heart was pounding so hard she could hardly breathe. She knew what he was going to ask, and this time she was ready. This time her answer would be yes, with no fear, no caution, no hesitation. This time she had had a month of lonely nights to think about it, and this time she wanted him as much as he wanted her.

"I want to marry you," he said.

Stunned, Laura pulled out of his arms and sat bolt upright. "What?" she cried, glaring at him.

Houston took a deep breath and repeated very clearly, "I want to marry you."

Laura closed her eyes and shook her head with a heavy sigh. When she was ready to kiss him, he wanted to make love to her. When she was ready to make love to him, he wanted to marry her. By the time she was ready to marry him, he'd probably be wanting to have kids.

Houston touched her arm consolingly. "You don't have to give me an answer. I wasn't even really proposing. I just wanted you to know how I feel."

Laura opened her eyes again and waved her hand in front of her face to help clear the confusion. "It's just that it wasn't what I was expecting you to say."

"I guess I kind of shocked you."

"A little."

"Well, I might as well scare you even worse." He leaned back, reached into his pocket and pulled out a little box. "Rebecca said I shouldn't do this. Jessica said she'd be flattered, but she'd probably make me exchange it."

He opened the box and held it out to her. Inside was a beautiful marquise-cut diamond solitaire of at least a carat and probably more. Laura reached for it, stopping herself just before she took it out of his hand. It was absolutely beautiful.

Wanting to take her mind off the temptation to try it on, she asked, "Who's Jessica?"

"My other sister. Rebecca's twin."

"She was right. I'm flattered." Flattered and tempted, but by the ring, not the proposal. She wasn't ready for marriage. She wasn't sure she would ever be ready for marriage.

"I bought it the day after Christmas."

"But Houston, isn't marriage awfully serious for people who've known each other such a short time? Do you realize this is our first date?"

He closed the ring box and put it on the edge of the coffee table. Then he stood and walked to the windows. Studying the view, he propped his forearm against the wall. His long, muscular body was relaxed.

"The day I met you," he said without turning, "something very different happened to me. I hardly knew you, and yet I felt like I'd known you forever."

He turned, then, and started walking toward her. "Sometimes, Laura, things happen that you can't explain or control. Sometimes logic just doesn't apply." He sat beside her and took both her hands in his. "I didn't plan for this to happen, but I'm willing to take a chance that we can make it work."

"I'm just not ready for marriage yet, Houston."

"I can understand that. Two months ago I wasn't, either." A slow smile spread over his face. "And then this green-eyed blonde came flying through the air and landed at my feet. And it seemed like every time I had myself almost talked out of falling in love with her, she got herself into some new kind of predicament. And I finally just said to myself, Houston, this woman needs you. Bad."

Trying not to laugh, Laura said, "Houston, you're skating on thin ice. Seriously."

He leaned back, still smiling. "So, if you weren't expecting me to say that I wanted to marry you, what were you expecting me to say?"

Unprepared for the rapid change of subject, Laura found herself stuttering. "That, well... That you wanted to, uh..."

"Sleep with you?"

She picked at the lacy ruffle on her skirt and carefully avoided looking directly at him. "Um, yes."

He covered her restless hands with his. "I do."

"Well," she said, throwing her hands up in exasperation, "now you've got me so confused." She stood, picked up a tray and started toward the kitchen.

Houston picked up another tray and followed her. There, he took both trays and set them on the counter. Then he took her by the hand and led her from the kitchen to the area between the kitchen and the bed. "I'm sorry I said anything about marriage." He slid his arms around her waist and pulled her to him. "I'm sorry I bought the ring. I've always been too impetuous, and I guess I still am. I didn't mean to make you unhappy."

"I don't think unhappy is the right word. I think it's more like nervous, maybe." But she didn't feel nervous anymore. She felt safe and comfortable in his arms. Being upset with Houston was like trying to stay mad at a puppy.

"Are you still nervous?"

"Well, I don't expect to be wearing the ring home tomorrow, if that's what you mean. But I think I can tolerate being in the same room with it so long as you keep the box closed."

"That's fair enough. And we'll just forget I ever brought it up."

"Thank you."

He slid his hand up her back and held her against his chest. "You know, Laura, I think I know something else that could be making you a little nervous."

"What's that?" she asked, fighting a strong impulse to pull away from him and put about half the room between them.

"I think it's being here with me, alone, so late at night, wondering what's going to happen next." His fingers slid through her hair and pulled her head back until she was staring into his eyes. His hand flattened on the back of her head, cradling it.

She watched his lips slowly lower toward hers, and the instant they touched, Laura felt herself relax in his arms. The night's fatigue, tension and fear blew away like smoke on the wind. All the longing, loneliness and desire she had ever felt for him were there and growing stronger with each second of his kiss.

"I think maybe it's time to stop talking," Houston said finally in a husky, honeyed drawl.

Laura wasn't sure she could talk so she just nodded. She was ready. Consciously, logically, physically and emotionally, she was ready. She wanted Houston more than she had ever wanted anybody, more than she had ever dreamed she could want anybody.

He lifted her in his arms and carried her to the bed while butterflies fluttered wildly inside her, half from fear and half from excitement.

"Don't be scared, princess," Houston whispered as he laid her on the bed. "It's a night made for fairy tales."

Her heart seemed to be blocking her throat, and her whole body throbbed to the rhythm of her pulse. "It's just that..." She suddenly choked on her own words.

Houston's hand slipped under her arm and smoothly unzipped her dress. He slid her shoes from her feet and set them on the floor at the side of the bed. Then he sat on the edge of the bed next to her and brushed a lock of hair away from her face.

"I know," he said softly. "It's your first time. I knew from our first kiss that you weren't someone who took love lightly. I told myself then that if I didn't really love you, I should leave you alone."

"Houston." She reached up and stroked his cheek. "I do love you. I really do. I love you so much."

He caught her hand in his and turned his head to kiss her palm. "Laura. My Laura."

He sat there with his lips pressed to her palm, not moving, not saying anything, until Laura touched his cheek and asked, "What's wrong?"

"I honestly don't know if I could stand to make love to you and then lose you."

Laura didn't know what to say. She was scared, and a small part of her mind still wanted to run and hide from the emotions he was arousing in her. But her body ached for him, had ached for him for weeks. Her body wanted his touch, needed him next to her, longed for the kind of feelings it had never known, feelings he alone could arouse in her.

"What do you want me to say?" she asked.

Houston stood, took her hand and helped her sit on the side of the bed. Then he sat beside her and said, "You and I have kept a secret from your father."

Laura nodded, and the dread that had been building receded a little. "If you want me to tell him, I was going to, anyway. I was just waiting until this apartment was ready."

"I'm glad you're going to, but that's not it."
Houston let his breath out in a long sigh and stared at
the floor. "There's something else that I've known
about, that I'm a part of, that your father asked me
not to tell you about. I kept quiet at first because I
thought it was between the two of you. And then I
kept quiet because I was afraid of how you would feel
about me if you knew. Now, I'm afraid to keep quiet
any longer."

Laura moved away just a little. "What is it?"

"Your father wants to sell the Polo Station."

Once more the night's conversation took a turn that
left her stunned. "The Groves? All of it?" She could
see her childhood, her last link with the happy memories, disappearing before her eyes.

He nodded. "All of it. Land, stables, horses, house,
the whole business, everything. He'd like to stay on as
manager of the business and to retain the house as his
home for his lifetime. Then everything would become
the new owner's."

"But why?" She had known things could never be
the way they used to be. She knew she would be leaving soon to build a life apart from Max's, but it still
hurt that he would sell the farm without telling her. It
hurt terribly.

Houston took her hands and held them in his own.
"A lot of reasons," he said gently. "I think it's partly
that he wants to see the Polo Station in the hands of
someone who'll carry on after he's gone."

"I guess Lorene and I don't exactly qualify."

"I'm pretty sure he's put most of his money into the
land, too. The money from the sale will give him
something to leave his heirs."

"What if his heirs don't want money?" Laura asked quietly.

"What do you think Lorene would prefer?"

She thought about it a minute. For Lorene, the past was a distant memory. She had a husband, and a baby on the way. She had a new life, and Max and the farm had no place in it.

"Money," she said finally, realizing that even if she wanted to argue, it would be futile.

"I'm sorry, Laura."

"It's not your fault. Lorene never cared about the land the way I did. But, Houston..." She turned to look at him and laid her hand on his arm. "Why did you think I'd be upset with you?"

He drew in a deep breath and stared straight ahead. "Because I'm the man who's going to buy it," he said clearly. "Your father offered it to me last spring." Slowly he turned toward her. "And I want it, Laura, very badly."

She stiffened, and anger began to burn in her chest. "My home?"

He reached for her, but she pulled away. Clasping her hands tightly in her lap, she put a wall between them.

"Try to understand, Laura," Houston said urgently. "I didn't even know you existed until last month."

She had never felt so betrayed. She had trusted him with her heart, and he had kept this from her since the day they had met. He had conspired with Max behind her back and had wooed her with meaningless generosity.

"No wonder you were so eager to help me get my business going," she said, her pain turning to anger. "Then you wouldn't have to feel so guilty about buying my home out from under me."

Wanting to put distance between them, she stood suddenly. At the movement, her unzipped dress parted, creating a wide gap. The loose, heart-shaped bodice slipped to reveal a glimpse of the black corset underneath before she grabbed the dress and held it closed.

"The house will be Max's for as long as he lives," Houston argued, his eyes following her as she paced in front of him. "And until then it would be as much your home as it is now."

"And then what?" Her anger flaring, she flung out her arm, and the dress slipped again. Growing as irritated with the dress as she was with Houston, Laura jerked it up with both hands. She stood, her elbows jutting awkwardly, while she held the dress closed and glared at Houston.

"And then," Houston snapped, losing his patience, "then you'd have a tidy little bundle of cash, is what. The place isn't going for peanuts, you know."

"Well, maybe I don't want cash." Nearly shouting, Laura jammed both fists down on her hips, and the dress slipped one more time. This time she let it, preferring to concentrate on the argument. "Maybe I'd rather have my home."

She turned angrily, and the bodice of the dress slid lower as she paced. In one smooth motion, the full skirt dipped to the floor and entangled with her ankles in midstride. Laura reached to pull the dress up at the same instant the toe of her shoe came down on the skirt and yanked it out of reach.

"In that case," Houston said quietly, "I told him I wouldn't buy it. I told him if you weren't happy about it, I wouldn't be a party to it."

While he spoke, Laura frantically groped for the dress, catching the bodice as it pooled around her ankles. Giving up, she stepped out of the dress and kicked it angrily into the air. She caught the dress on its way down and stood with it dangling from her hand as Houston's words sank in.

"You said that?" she asked, beginning to feel a little foolish after her outburst.

"Yes, I did. The very day I met you."

Moved, she took a step toward him. "Houston." Then she realized that he was looking everywhere but at her. Glancing down, she saw black underwear, very little of it, and nothing else, and she hastily clutched the dress in front of her.

"What did he say to that?" she asked, curiosity quickly outweighing embarrassment.

"He said he'd find another buyer." Houston rubbed his hand across his forehead and finally allowed himself to look at her. "I'll be honest with you, Laura. I get the feeling sometimes that what he really wants is to make sure none of you can move there after he's gone. You know Max. He's no angel."

"No, he's no angel." It sounded so like her father. Only Max would arrange to take the fight with him to the grave.

"Are you still mad at me?" Houston asked.

"No, I'm not mad at you." Now that she was calmer, she was beginning to wonder how long she was going to have to stand there holding her dress in front of her.

He grinned. "Want to come a little closer and prove it?"

"That depends," Laura said, returning his mischievous smile. "Have you got any more confessions to make?"

"That was the last one."

She took a step toward him and stopped as a new thought struck her. "Oh, Houston, Max is going to be so mad when he finds out you've done all this without telling him." She waved her arm to encompass the apartment and the rooms beyond.

Houston smiled even more widely and nodded. "I may have to move in here with you."

Laura blushed. "Houston."

He reached out and caught her hand, guiding her toward him. "Laura." When she was near enough, he pulled her onto his lap and wrapped his arms around her.

"Oh, Houston." Her arms went around his neck, and she laid her cheek against his.

"I wonder if we can remember where we were before I gave in to my fit of confession," he teased, lifting her hand and kissing the palm.

"I think I was lying down," Laura offered helpfully.

"And I was trying to figure out a way to get this the rest of the way off," he said, touching the dress that was crumpled between them.

"I guess you feel pretty clever, then, don't you?" Laura retorted. She was feeling wanton and shy at the same time, and she was infinitely grateful for the depth of night that surrounded them.

The smaller candles had long since flickered and gone out. The tapers were burning low. Moonlight glowed through the tall, uncurtained windows, lighting the near half of the room and leaving the bed in shadow,

"I'd feel a lot more clever if you weren't still holding on to it," he said, and rubbed the lace of the skirt between his fingers.

Feeling bold beyond measure, Laura took the dress by the bodice, pulled it out from between them and dropped it onto the rug beside the bed.

Outside, the night had grown silent. Inside, the only sound was their breathing.

"Laura," Houston whispered.

His hand moved up her arm, leaving goose bumps where he touched. At her shoulder, his thumb stroked over her skin and along her collarbone. His other hand covered her other shoulder. His thumb traced the outline of her collarbone until the fingers of both hands were splayed at the base of her neck and his thumbs touched at the hollow of her throat. Slowly his thumbs spread out, stroking the top of her breasts, and the tension in Laura's stomach coiled into a tight, tingly knot.

She caught her breath, inhaling in short, uneven gasps. She closed her eyes and felt her neck arch.

"Your skin's so soft," he said quietly. "So smooth."

Her shyness all but vanished, Laura felt the wanton in her blossom at his touch. She loved the slow, sure exploration of his hands. She loved that he was the first.

"Do you wear things like this often?" Houston asked, running the tip of his finger over the low, lacy edge of the corset.

Laura caught her breath in a long, deep sigh as his finger left the fabric and made the return trip across her skin.

"Never," she said in a husky voice she hardly recognized.

"I like it a lot," he answered.

Before she could say anything else, he leaned over and pressed his lips to the base of her throat. His teeth nipped at her skin in gentle pricks that sent cold chills down her back.

She gasped, then released her breath in a soft moan as his tongue stroked her neck where his teeth had been. Involuntarily her fingers curled against his back, and she clutched his shirt in her fists.

"Laura, Laura," he sighed against her neck. His slow kisses trailed down her throat and into the valley between her breasts. "You're so much more than I ever imagined," he whispered, his breath hot and moist against her skin.

Her breath came in gasps. Her heart was wild inside her chest. Feelings she had never known pounded at her as he pressed his lips against the lace that covered her breasts.

She could feel the heat of his embrace burning inside her. Her fingers wound through his hair while his hands molded her sides, then moved to the garter belt just below her waist, then to the thin slice of skin between the garter belt and her bikini pants.

When he moved to the bare thigh between her bikinis and the lace top of her hose, Laura's entire body quivered. His hand moved deeper, stroking the inside of her thigh, then higher, brushing the silk-covered cleft between her legs.

Shocked by the intensity of her arousal, Laura cried out, pulled away and stumbled to her feet.

"Laura, sweetheart, what is it?" Concerned, Houston stood and caught her arms to steady her. "Did I scare you? Am I going too fast?"

She stared at him, quaking with a need that was stronger than her fear. "I never knew it could feel like this."

He pulled her close and brushed her hair with a kiss. "Then you don't want me to stop?"

"I don't think I could stand it if you did," she said, shivering in his arms.

Houston stepped back, and with hands that were none too steady, he quickly unbuttoned his shirt and wrapped it around her shoulders. "We'd better get you under the covers."

Laura watched as he pulled back the spread, turned down the sheet and swept the extra pillows onto the floor. Then he took her hand and led her to the bed. Almost helpless from the storm of emotions raging in her, she sank gratefully onto the side of the bed.

While he competently unhooked her stockings from her garters, she couldn't help wondering just how much experience he had. His hands were sure and tantalizingly tender as he rolled her stockings down her legs one by one. He lingered at her ankles before he slid the stockings from her feet.

Laura's heart was pounding wildly, and her shivers were gone by the time he dropped his shirt to the floor and reached behind her to unhook her corset. His lips were next to her ear, and his bare chest brushed hers, the heated scent of pure male mingling with the crisp tang of cologne.

Her hands touched his sides and slid down to mold his waist, feeling the supple flexing of his muscles against her palms as he worked to free the last hooks at the waist of her corset.

Moving lower, he freed the fastening of the garter belt, and when he stepped back, he brought them both with him. Clad in nothing but her bikini underwear, Laura felt a powerful mingling of sensuality and vulnerability. She was suddenly aware of her body as she had never been.

Houston knelt on one knee and took her hands in his. "Are you still cold?" he asked softly.

Her skin burned. She was on fire. Her whole body felt heavy with desire. "No," she said in a voice thickened by emotion.

He kissed her hands, rose and kissed her on the lips quickly, then again, harder. "Don't move. I'll be right back."

Feeling deserted, Laura turned and followed him to the bathroom with her eyes. When the door closed behind him, she turned her gaze to the windows.

The moon was high, and the light that flowed through was diffused to a soft glow. The candles had burned down, and their light was gone, leaving the room with nothing but the moonlight.

In the quiet, Laura could almost hear the pounding of her heart, quick and steady. Alone, she tried to think, to cool the fever pitch of her emotions, but the volcano burning inside her was white hot. She had never felt this way before, but she knew what she felt was true.

She was in love, and wisely or unwisely, she was about to consummate that love. And she had never been surer about anything in her life.

The bathroom door opened, and she turned toward it as Houston emerged and started across the room. Even in the dark, she could see the subtle changes in his skin tones. His arms were darkest, then his chest, and his legs gleamed almost as white against the darkness as her skin did.

She'd seen nudes in books. She'd seen nude men in movies and almost-nude men at the beach. But she'd never seen a man totally nude in person until now, and she was almost afraid to look.

He was halfway across the room when she began to walk toward him, and they met at the side of the bed. He tossed the towel he was carrying onto the middle of the bed and swept her against him.

"I was almost afraid you might change your mind while I was gone," he said, running his hand over the smooth skin of her back. "Any second thoughts?"

His hand rested on the curve of her hip, not quite touching the top of her bikini briefs. Her breasts were crushed against his chest. She could almost feel the beating of his heart next to hers.

She tilted her head and gazed at his face, just visible in the pale light. "My second thoughts are the same as my first."

"You don't know how glad I am to hear that." His thumb slid under the edge of her bikinis, and his mouth lowered to hers, touching gently, tenderly, then growing more demanding.

His arms tightened around her, and his whole body grew taut. Enveloped in the hard press of his powerful muscles, she felt lost in the kiss that grew deeper, harder and more searching.

Laura felt alive with heightened sensations as the coarse feathering of hair on his legs brushed the smooth skin on hers. Her breasts were welded to the velvety warmth of his chest. Her heart accelerated wildly at the faint throb she felt pressed against her stomach.

Houston's hand slid inside her bikinis and tugged gently downward. Laura slipped her hand in the other side, and together they eased the underwear over her hips and down her thighs. When the pants dropped to the floor, she stepped out of them, and without another word Houston lifted her into his arms and set her on the bed.

Lying beside her, he held himself over her on one elbow and stared at her. With his fingertips, he lightly stroked her neck, across her shoulder and down to follow the outside curve of her breast. When he reached its base, he cupped the weight of her breast in his hand and lifted it toward him as he leaned to take the tip gently into his mouth.

Laura moaned softly, and her eyelids fluttered shut. Eddies of pleasure coursed through her. The soft tugging at her breast sent electric tingles from the pit of her stomach down the insides of her thighs.

Twisting against the aching ecstasy that seemed to be everywhere, she gasped at the feel of his hand on her waist. His palm slid over the flat of her stomach and into the valley between her legs. His finger stroked the softly pulsing flesh that was sheltered there while his mouth lifted from one breast and moved to the other, and the intensity of the pleasure he gave her went beyond endurance.

"Houston, please," Laura whispered, "please."

His kiss trailed from the aching peak of her breast to her throat, leaving a trail of flame where his lips touched. He slid his hands under her hips and lifted her onto the towel. As he lowered her again, his tongue flicked at her lips, darting between them, driving deep into the interior of her mouth then withdrawing.

He covered her mouth with his, kissing her softly, while he slid his body over hers, coming to rest between her legs.

When the kiss ended and he stared into her eyes, Laura knew the moment had come. Once it was done, it could never be undone, and she would never be the same again. She would belong to Houston in a way she had never belonged to anyone. And he would belong to her, and whatever happened, that bond between them would always be there.

"I love you, Laura," Houston said in a voice that sounded strained beyond measure.

Frightened more by the emotions gone wild inside her than by what was about to happen, Laura put her heart in his hands. "And I love you."

She was ready. She wanted him more than she had imagined she could. In open invitation she edged nearer to the hard, swollen pressure against the inside of her thigh.

In answer, Houston guided himself toward her then paused. Her heart pounding in her throat, Laura shifted her weight and felt him slide like velvet past the edge of the opening and stop just inside.

They both gasped, and Houston lowered his forehead to hers, holding perfectly still while he caught his breath. Then he moved deeper in short, slow circles that only added to the sweet torment that was building in them both. Finally, in one long stroke he broke the thin barrier and held her tightly through her sudden flash of pain.

Gently, he began to move again, deep within her, withdrawing slowly, then entering, building in speed and passion until they were both lost in the power of their feelings, blind and deaf to everything but the dance that brought them to the edge and into the yawning gulf beyond.

Breathing as deeply as if she'd run a marathon, Laura lay quietly in Houston's arms. She kissed his shoulder and slowly stroked her fingertips over his chest, feeling happiness and contentment that were complete. She knew what love felt like, and she knew she could never go back to the way her life had been.

The only life she could imagine now was with Houston.

His arms tightened around her, and he pressed his lips to her temple in a long, tender kiss. "How do you feel about kids?" he asked softly.

Hearing her prediction come true, Laura couldn't help laughing. "Let's just get the wedding over with first, okay?"

His kiss moved lower, traveling across her cheek and the bridge of her nose and down the other cheek to her mouth. "A big one or a little one?"

"A little one." She chuckled and stared at the canopy overhead. "I can't believe I'm talking about this."

"Neither can I, but before you change your mind..." He pulled his arm from under her and walked quickly to the coffee table, returning with the ring.

Lying beside her, he lifted her hand and said solemnly, "Laura, will you marry me?" He held the ring poised over her left ring finger.

Laura looked at him and felt a swelling of love so strong it hurt to breathe. "Yes. Oh, yes."

He slipped the ring on her finger and gathered her into his arms again, holding her to him fiercely while their love blended into passion and their thoughts of tomorrow evaporated into the urgency of the night.

Chapter Ten

Winter had returned overnight. Laura shivered as she stepped out of the car in front of her father's house.

"I'd offer you my jacket if I had one," Houston said. He wrapped his arm around her shoulders to give her what warmth he could.

"I think it's more nerves than anything." She looked from the house to the ring on her finger. Holding out her hand, she watched the diamond glitter in the bright afternoon sun. She was about to announce her engagement to her family and meet Houston's sister for the first time, and she was still wearing the strapless dress she'd been wearing when she'd left the house the night before. She couldn't help feeling a little like a teenager sneaking in after curfew with her sweater buttoned wrong.

Houston hugged her to him and gave her a reassuring kiss on her forehead, and in an instant her jitters were gone. She was in love. She was engaged. She didn't know how it had happened, but she wanted to tell the world about it.

"Any regrets?" he asked, his voice warm and comforting close to her ear.

She gazed at him in unblushing adoration. "Only that I didn't meet you sooner."

He smiled and held her tighter. "That's the kind of talk I like to hear."

"And that I didn't think to bring a change of clothes," she added, casting another worried glance at the house.

"But then I might think you'd planned for us to spend the night together."

Vixenish, she looked at him through her lashes. "Maybe I did."

"Did you really?"

"Well, maybe not planned, exactly, but I was considering the possibility."

Houston sighed and put both arms around her, pulling her against his stomach. "I'm going to hate having to share you with other people today."

"I know. But we have to sooner or later."

"So it might as well be now," he agreed reluctantly.

Slowly, with their arms around each other's waists, they walked up the front steps, across the wide terrace and through the front door.

"Well, hello there, you two," Julia called from the living room. "We're in here."

Julia and Rebecca were sitting opposite each other on the matching sofas. Laura peeked into the corner as she entered the room, and was relieved to find that Max's desk was unoccupied.

"He's down at the stables, I think," Julia said. "And Rebecca and I have just been sitting here passing the time in speculation."

His hand still on Laura's waist, Houston stopped at the end of the sofa and sat casually on its arm. "Laura, this is my sister Rebecca. Rebecca, this is the love of my life, Laura."

Laura reached across Houston and took Rebecca's hand, automatically looking for a family resemblance. Rebecca's hair was darker than Houston's. It was long and thick and shiny. Her eyes were brown, wider and rounder than Houston's. "How do you do?" she said, and gave up on finding any similarities.

"It's a real pleasure to meet you, Laura." Rebecca's voice was soft and sweet, and she seemed a little shy. "I've heard a lot about you."

"I'm almost afraid to ask this," Houston said to Julia, with a sidelong glance at his sister, "but what were you two speculating about?"

"Oh," Julia said with an airy flutter of her hand, "about what Max is thinking, and about what you've been doing, and about what Max is thinking you've been doing."

"Well..." Laura hedged. Without Max to worry about, her enjoyment outweighed her anxiety. She laid her hand over Houston's, which was on top of his knee, and casually exposed the gleaming diamond to view.

Rebecca gasped and let out a happy cry. "Oh, no. You don't mean it. Houston, I'm so happy for you." She jumped to her feet and threw her arms around her brother's shoulders.

While Houston suffered his sister's congratulations, Julia walked over and lifted Laura's hand. She looked from the ring to Laura's face in wonderment. "I guess this means he really liked the dress," she said finally.

Rebecca reached across Houston to touch Laura's arm. "Oh, Laura, I'm just thrilled about this."

"Thank you," Laura said, warming rapidly to her future sister-in-law. There was a warmth and openness about Rebecca that reminded her a great deal of Houston. She wondered if his whole family was the same way and what it would feel like after the painfully guarded emotions she had grown used to in her own family.

She turned to Julia and quietly asked, "You're not upset, are you?" She had expected disapproval from Max, but not from her mother.

Julia smiled and took her daughter's face between her hands. "Oh, no, baby, not at all. I'm very happy. I just didn't expect the two of you to come home engaged after your first date. I expected something maybe a little slower. Didn't you, Rebecca?"

Rebecca grinned. "Well, actually, yes."

Laura looked at Houston and felt the same way he had earlier. She would have given anything to be alone with him. Already it seemed she had known him forever. It was hard to believe last night had been their first date. She touched her ring and smiled softly. "I guess a lot of us are a little surprised."

"About what?" Max demanded from the door-way.

"Well," Julia said, popping up from the couch and holding out her hand to Rebecca, "I promised to show Rebecca the garden." She herded the puzzled but obedient Rebecca ahead of her toward the door. "We'll be back in a little while," she called over her shoulder.

Max rolled himself into the room and wheeled around to face Laura and Houston. "Sit down, both of you," he snapped. "You know how I hate having to stare up at people."

Girding herself for the storm that was about to break, Laura took Rebecca's place on the sofa and Houston slid in beside her. She slipped her hand under his and squeezed tightly, drawing comfort and hiding the engagement ring at the same time.

Max glared at them in silence, gathering strength. Laura recognized a tirade building. Houston's hand moved on hers, reminding her silently that she wasn't alone, and Laura felt herself relax.

"Well," Max finally said, "what have you got to say for yourselves? Since it's obvious to everyone that you spent the night together."

"Max, I realize Laura's your daughter," Houston said quietly. "But I love her, and I'm going to marry her, and I want you to be very careful what you say."

"Marry her!" Max exploded. The knuckles on his hands turned white where he gripped the wheels of his chair. "You hardly know her!"

"Nevertheless," Houston said evenly, "I've asked her to marry me, and she's consented."

Max leaned forward, his face twitching with anger. "And just how much does she know about you? Did you tell her about our little deal? Or were you hoping she wouldn't find out about your part in that?"

Laura closed her eyes and gave silent thanks for Houston's honesty. She knew her father's version could have been devastating.

Houston's hand tightened on hers again in a reassuring squeeze, and he answered calmly, "Yes, she knows."

Not satisfied, Max straightened in his wheelchair and tilted his head in a familiar pose of arrogance. "And has it occurred to you that she's only marrying you to keep her land?"

"Max, give it up," Houston snapped, his patience at an end. "You're not going to drive a wedge between us. And you're only going to make yourself look bad by trying."

His anger unabated, Max turned his fury from Houston to Laura. "And how long has this little affair been going on? How long have you and my so-called friend been sneaking around behind my back?"

She hadn't expected him to be fair or reasonable or even just a little happy for her. But he was still her father, and as hard as she tried not to be hurt by his petty attack, Laura felt tears burning in her eyes as Houston bolted to his feet.

"That's enough!" he shouted. "You can level on me all you want to, but you leave her alone."

Max leaned as far forward as he could and answered through clenched teeth. "She's my daughter, and I'll talk to her any way I damn well please. You're the outsider here, and I'll thank you to remember it."

Laura turned her back to Max and said in a low voice, "We're not getting anywhere like this. I think I should talk to him alone."

Houston squared his shoulders. "I don't want to leave you."

"He's just going to get angrier. And I might as well tell him about the rest of it."

"I won't be far." Houston swept past Max and out of the room.

Laura sat on the edge of the sofa and looked her father in the eye. "I have something else to tell you that you may not want to hear."

Max slapped the arms of his wheelchair and leaned back defiantly. "Fire away."

"You may have been too sick to remember this, but I sold my tearooms in Arkansas when I came here last year, because I was planning to stay. Then when you got better, I realized you didn't need me. You already had a life that you were content with, and there was no place for me in it. So I decided it was time for me to get on with my own life."

Max glared but stayed quiet, and she continued. "I've taken a long-term lease on two floors of a building on River Street." He began to puff up, and she held up her hand to stop whatever he was about to say. "I'd started this long before I met Houston, so I don't want you trying to twist this and make it his fault."

"I never expected you to spend your life playing nursemaid to me," Max said gruffly. "Why did you think I'd get mad about you starting up another business?"

"Because the hours are going to be too long for me to drive back and forth every day. There's an apartment in the building I've already had renovated for me."

"So you were leaving me," he said with a sullen glare. "Even before Houston, you were already making plans to leave."

She looked at him and wondered if there was anything she could say that would get through to him. He didn't want her to stay, and he didn't want her to go. He didn't want to be a father to her, but he was furious with Houston for wanting to marry her. She didn't know what he wanted. She didn't know if he knew.

"Nothing I do is ever enough, is it?" Suddenly shouting, Max lunged forward in his wheelchair. "I bet you wonder why I was going to sell this place, don't you? Well, that's why." He pounded the arm of his chair, his face growing flushed. "I knew you were leaving again. I didn't know when, and I didn't know what excuse you'd use, but I knew you'd leave. You're just like your mother."

He drew in a long breath and leaned back. Laura held herself in check. Maybe after he had shouted himself out, he would be calm enough to listen to her.

His voice almost a hiss, Max went on, "And the first time Houston's down and out, are you going to leave him too? Well, don't come running to me, little girl, you hear me?" He clutched the arms of the wheelchair and lunged forward again. "Because you're not welcome here. This isn't your home anymore. Not now, not ever again. I want you and your lover out of here today." He was shouting and his shaking arm pointed to the door. "Before the sun sets, you hear? Both of you. And his sister, and your mother. All of you! Out!"

"Now, hold on just a minute, Max," Julia said coolly as she marched into the room and into the middle of the fray. "This house is as much mine as it is yours until a judge says different. I'm not leaving here until I'm damned good and ready. And neither is Laura, or Houston, or Rebecca. And if you can't behave yourself, you can just go out to the guest lodge and stay there until you calm down. And that, as they say back home, is how the cow ate the cabbage."

Furious, Max drove his wheelchair past Julia and through the doorway, where Houston stood. He stopped and wheeled to face Houston. "You can forget the deal. You'll get this place over my dead body. I'd give it away to a stranger before I'd let you have it."

Into the stunned silence following his departure, Julia said, "Well, hasn't this been a lovely start to the new year?"

Houston went to Laura and pulled her into his arms. "Oh, baby, I'm so sorry. I should never have left you alone with him."

She leaned her head on his shoulder and tried not to cry. "He's been like that since the accident. We're used to it."

"How could anyone ever get used to that?"

Grateful just to have him near, Laura curled tighter in his embrace. She was starting a new life, a better, happier life with a man who wasn't afraid to love and be loved. "Oh, Houston," she whispered, "hold me. Just hold me, and don't ever let me go."

* * *

Houston gazed at the book of china patterns Laura held half in her lap and half in his and tried not to squirm.

"Honey, are you sure this is something I'm really supposed to care about?" he asked uncertainly.

Julia smiled, leaned over and patted his hand. "I think it's one of those things that you're not going to care about unless she picks the wrong one."

They were just plates. Nobody actually looked at plates. They were always covered up by food. Perplexed, he looked from Julia to Laura. "Couldn't we just get plain white? Maybe with one of those little gold band things around the outside?"

Laura looked at him the way he imagined she might look at a dead fish she was going to have to clean, so he guessed plain white was out. "Why don't you just pick something you like, sweetheart," he coaxed. "I'm sure I'll like it just fine."

She smiled and said in a soft, sweet voice tempered with steel, "You're going to have to eat off of them, too, dear. If you'll just point out a few that you really like and show me which ones you really hate, I'll do all the rest."

"Okay, sweetheart," Houston agreed without hesitation.

He knew when he had pushed her patience far enough. Getting a business going and a marriage arranged at the same time couldn't be easy, especially with a mother who wanted everything done right and a father who didn't want anything done at all.

Laura relaxed and gave him a grateful peck on the cheek. Then she smiled at him and nuzzled closer. Impetuously, Houston caught her chin in his hand and returned her affection with a quick kiss on the lips that would have grown into a lot more if they'd been alone.

Houston sat close to Laura for an hour, liking and disliking a multitude of patterns that he would never recognize if he saw them again. Eventually the choices were narrowed down to half a dozen patterns that he would be more than happy to eat from for the rest of his life, and Laura closed the book with a satisfied smile.

"Thank you, darling," she said with her beautiful green bedroom eyes gazing at him lovingly. "The crystal won't be nearly as hard, I promise."

The panic he felt must have shown in his eyes, because she laughed and quickly added, "Not now. We're through for today."

Rebecca looked up from her needlework. "You're through so soon?"

Laura stacked the last book on top of the others. "He was wonderful," Laura told her. "Our tastes even match, once I got him past that all-white business."

Rebecca smiled at him proudly. "I always thought he was pretty wonderful. The problem with Houston is that he's made it awfully hard for other men to measure up."

"Please, please, I can't take any more of this." Houston laughingly held up his hands in protest.

"Neither can I," Max said, entering midway through the praise.

"Max," everyone said at once, and turned toward him.

The scene of New Year's Day had blown over, and a truce had been established. Max had apologized to

Laura and had halfheartedly reinstated his offer to
Houston, but there was a nervous expectation that
seemed to fill the air whenever he entered a room.
Houston could feel it now, as if everyone was still
waiting for another bomb to drop.

"And what are we doing today?" Max asked.

"Picking china patterns," Julia answered.

They were like two combatants circling each other,
polite but wary. Houston tried to imagine the kind of
couple they had once been. Occasionally he thought
he could almost see a spark of love flash between
them, but it was hard to believe that once they must
have been as young and happy and wildly in love as he
and Laura were.

"Well, Houston, I've come to rescue you from all
this with the announcement of a little sporting event
I've arranged in your honor," Max announced with
rare good humor. "Sort of an engagement celebration and bachelor party all in one."

"What sort of a sporting event?" Julia asked. Her
eyes narrowed cautiously as she waited for his answer.

"A polo match, of course. An invitational exhibi-
tion polo match, with Houston as captain of the Station team."

"How wonderful," Rebecca said enthusiastically.
"I used to help arrange some of the charity matches
back home. I'd love to help with this one."

Houston looked at his radiant sister and wished it
was that simple. He felt ice in his veins when his gaze
traveled from Rebecca to Laura, who sat beside him
like a stone statue.

It was the one thing they hadn't discussed. He had been so busy with the renovations and the wedding plans, he had barely had time to think about polo, never mind resolve the problem that Laura detested the game as passionately as he loved it.

"Augh!" The sound exploded out of Max, and he slammed his hand on the arm of his wheelchair. "You're all sitting around here like sticks of wood. It won't be much more than a practice game with some local players and clinic students. Just a little harmless fun. Besides, I've already made all the arrangements."

"Excuse me," Laura said almost inaudibly.

She stood and brushed by Houston before he could stop her. When he started after her, Julia held up her hand to stop him.

"Let me," she said. She paused beside Max and shook her head in annoyance. "Honestly, Max."

"Well, it's got to happen sometime," he said, "unless Houston's planning to give up polo."

"Did it have to happen now?" she asked, unconvinced.

"When's a better time? After the wedding?"

"I think I hate it most when you're right," Julia fumed, and strode out of the room, abandoning her usual slow grace.

"You could have said something to me about it first, Max," Houston said quietly.

"It was supposed to be a surprise. If you talk about surprises first, they're not surprises."

Once more, Houston felt caught in a struggle that wasn't his own. He agreed with Max, but he sympathized with Laura. And he definitely didn't like Max's high-handed actions.

"If you talk about surprises first, maybe they don't happen at all," he said sternly, "which is exactly what may happen here."

"What are you going to do, Houston? Buy this place and watch other people play polo? Are you planning to give the game up totally?" Max challenged. "Or maybe you're hoping some morning you're going to wake up and, like magic, Laura isn't going to be afraid anymore."

Houston shook his head. "I should have discussed it with her first. We haven't talked about it since we were engaged. You shouldn't have sprung it on her like that."

"The question is, now that I have, what are you going to do? Do you roll over and play dead for the rest of your life? Or do you get it straightened out now while there's still time?"

With that, Max turned and wheeled away. Houston had forgotten there was anyone else in the room until Rebecca said, "Wow. What a hornet's nest. What's going on?"

He turned slowly, Max's words still ringing in his ears, words that had the harsh sound of truth, but words that didn't change the way Laura felt.

"To make a long and unhappy story short, Max was paralyzed in a polo accident, and Laura was watching when it happened."

"Oh, how awful," Rebecca said, cringing while her soft brown eyes grew bigger and sadder. "And now she's afraid for you."

He nodded. "That's part of it. But Max's personality changed after the accident. He withdrew from his family. He and his wife separated. She and the girls moved away."

Rebecca took his hand sympathetically. "Julia told me some of it. I didn't realize it was a polo accident that started it all, though."

"I just don't know what I'm going to do."

"I know that in every marriage some compromises are necessary." She shook her head. "But in this case it's hard to know who should compromise. If I know you, you'll take up something like skydiving if you give up polo. That's just the way you are."

He looked into the brown eyes that had always told him the truth, even if it was a truth he didn't want to hear. "But am I wrong? Should I try to change?"

"Ah, Houston." Rebecca cocked her head. "I'll tell you about this guy I knew in college. He was one of the gentlest people I've ever met. But he was a football player, and in a game he became an animal. It was something I couldn't understand, so I asked him about it. He stood there and looked at me for a minute, then he said that maybe it was being so aggressive on the football field that allowed him to be so different off it."

She sighed and looked at Houston. "I lost touch with him after college, but I've often wondered what he's like now that he isn't playing anymore."

Houston touched her chin with his finger and smiled. "That's a very subtle warning, sister dear."

"Just a thought, my gentle brother. Just a thought."

"Well, I think I'll go find my bride now and see what she thinks about it."

Rebecca smiled and waved. "Good luck."

"The two of you haven't discussed this?" Julia asked gently.

"No." Laura twisted the engagement ring on her finger and watched the light dance in its depths.

"Does Houston know how you feel?" Julia paused a minute then took Laura's hand in hers. "Honey, there's a lot we've never really talked about. So maybe now it's time we did. Can you tell me why you're so against polo?"

Tears swam in Laura's eyes as she looked up at her mother in disbelief. "How can you ask that? It crippled Daddy. It ruined our lives."

"But, darling..." Julia patted Laura's hands consolingly while she searched for words. "Your father still loves it very much. He's built his whole life around it. Any kind of accident could have crippled him. It just happened to be during a polo game. And if anything ruined our lives, it was Max. He wasn't an easy man to live with before the accident, and he was impossible after it."

The tears Laura had been holding back began to slide silently down her cheeks. "I can't help it. I can't think of Houston out there without thinking of what could happen." She felt as if she was recounting a nightmare, and she couldn't seem to get her voice above a whisper. "I keep seeing him lying there like Daddy, not moving, and I just can't stand it."

The vision was clear in her mind. The old and the new. The reality and the possibility. The two men, so different and yet so much alike.

The tears kept coming, and Julia gathered Laura into her arms and held her while Laura cried the tears she had never shed as a child.

While her father had hovered between life and death, she had hidden her terror from everyone, afraid in her child's mind that somehow her fear could hurt her father. Afraid that her own weakness could cause him to grow weak and die, she had held her tears inside and had shown only her strength, holding it in front of him like a talisman to lead him toward life and health.

"I understand how you feel, honey," Julia crooned softly as she rocked Laura in her arms. "But you have to let the past go and think about the future. If Houston loves polo enough to want to buy this place and make it his life, think of what it would mean to him to have to give it up."

Laura lifted her head, tears streaming down her face. "But if anything happened to him, what would I do? If the same thing happened to us that happened to you and Daddy, I'd never forgive myself."

"Laura, baby, Max did it all by himself. He was so afraid I was going to leave him that he ended up driving me away."

"That doesn't make any sense."

"No, it doesn't," her mother said sadly. "And that's the part that used to make me so mad. I can't tell you the nights I've cried myself to sleep, praying that he would call and ask me to come back."

"Oh, Mom, I'm so sorry." It was Laura's turn to console her mother. "I wish I'd known. There were times I should have been nicer to you. I just never knew that you missed him as much as I did."

"Well, I did. And I still do." Julia smoothed Laura's hair away from her face. Then she looked her daughter in the eye and said, "Baby, listen to a woman who knows. Don't let your fear come between you and the man you love. Don't make Houston pay for your father's sins. Let him be what he is and stand by him no matter what happens. I should never have left your father. I know that now. I hoped it would bring him to his senses, and all it did was make him more bitter than ever."

"Oh, Mom, I love you." Laura held her mother tightly, wishing they hadn't waited so many years to talk. They all carried scars, and maybe with enough love and enough time they could find a way to put the past behind them.

Over her mother's shoulder, Laura saw Houston enter the room. She held out her hand to him.

Sensing his presence, Julia relinquished Laura into his arms. "I think I'll leave you two alone now. Just in case you have something to talk about."

"I'm sorry, baby," Houston said as soon as they were alone. "I had no idea he was going to do something like that."

"It's okay." She was so happy to see him, she didn't think there was anything he could do that would upset her.

"I'm not going to lie to you," he said. "It wouldn't be easy for me to give it up, but if it's that important to you, I'd try."

She shook her head. "It's okay."

"I could point out, though, that I haven't gotten into nearly as much trouble playing polo as you do on an average ride through the woods."

"You're right." She nodded in perfect agreement. "And it's okay with me if you want to play."

"And cars," he went on, not even hearing her. "The very thought of you behind the wheel of a car... What do you mean, it's okay?"

"You can play. It's all right. I'm not upset."

"You're not?"

"No." She smiled. "Rebecca's right. It could be a lot of fun. We could make it a real social event."

"What did your mother say?" he asked, bewildered by the dramatic change.

"Just something I should have been able to figure out for myself. You're not my father, and I don't have to be afraid of history repeating itself."

"I could have told you that."

"It wouldn't have had the same effect," Laura teased. "She cried."

"I can cry."

"Save it for another time," she said, nestling happily in his arms.

He began to smile. "Gladly. Now that we're finally alone, I can think of much better things for us to do."

Laura laughed. "I love a man with an imagination."

Chapter Eleven

Houston kissed Laura lightly on the mouth and gave her a quick, heartfelt hug. "Now, don't worry," he said.

"Right. Sure," Laura answered dryly, trying not to show the despair she felt.

"I have to go now, sweetheart," he said, gently disengaging himself from her arms. "You'll take care of her?" he asked Julia. He looked from her to Rebecca, then to Jessy, who had flown in for the event.

Julia slipped her arm around Laura's shoulders. "She'll be just fine."

Laura reached out to Houston as he began to leave. He caught her hand in his and held it as he backed away, his fingers slowly slipping through hers until he was out of reach. Then he turned and walked quickly away, and Laura closed her eyes and tried to hold back her tears.

"Sweetheart," Julia crooned, "nothing's going to happen to him."

"I know," Laura said in a raspy whisper.

But as hard as she tried to get it out of her mind, she kept seeing her father's accident. The horse stumbling, her father cartwheeling over the horse's shoulder, the long moment when he seemed suspended in air, then the landing. She had lost sight of him for an instant among the horses' hooves. Going too fast to stop, the ponies had veered around him, some jumping over him where there was no room to go around. And in a matter of seconds it was all over.

One horse had accidently clipped Max's shoulder and knocked him into the path of another horse that otherwise would have missed him cleanly. The horse's hoof had landed squarely on Max's back, snapping it.

She had only to walk onto a polo field to relive it all. The shocked gasp of the crowd as the people rose to their feet. The hush while they waited for the rider to move. The whispers when the stretcher came onto the field and carried Max away.

A terrible tragedy. A freak accident. So sorry. Hazard of the sport. Words, just empty words. Condolences that meant nothing, like the assurances that Houston would be all right. In her mind Laura knew nothing would happen to him, but in her heart she wouldn't relax until it was over.

"I know how you feel," Jessy said, taking her hand and helping Julia to steer Laura toward their seats. "I've been watching Houston do stuff like this since I was a little girl. I think I've logged more time with my heart in my throat than in my chest, thanks to him. And I've told him about it, too, but it hasn't made the slightest impression. And then he has the nerve to call me reckless."

"You are reckless, Jessy," Rebecca said with a laugh. "Poor Laura, I'm afraid you've gotten engaged into a family of lunatics."

Laura smiled and felt herself relaxing just a little. In the month and a half since Houston had returned with Rebecca, she had become very fond of her future sister-in-law. Watching the quiet heartbreak that Rebecca almost succeeded in hiding had helped Laura appreciate how truly lucky she was to have Houston.

"Now, Becky, watch it," Jessy said with a bubbly laugh. Her light, springy step carried her ahead, and she turned to face them, walking backward as she talked. "Laura might take you seriously. And if she's going to be our sister-in-law, we want her to at least start off with a good impression of us."

Laura smiled and thought that she had a pretty good impression based on the Carders she had met so far. Forceful, individual, kind and caring were the traits she had noticed most.

But she was having trouble accepting that Jessy and Rebecca were twins. One had the kind of quiet, dignified, dark beauty that made Laura think of a heroine in a Gothic romance. The other reminded her of champagne bubbles and butterfly wings and a golden-maned filly running free on a warm summer's day.

At the moment the fragile blossoming of mother-hood and the slow mending of a broken heart had combined to surround Rebecca with a delicately tragic air. But that was only temporary. Already Laura could see the wounded spirit healing and strengthening and the true Rebecca emerging.

And in Jessy she could sense the same nurturing instincts that were so strong in Houston. But instead of lavishing those instincts on the world the way Houston did, Jessy seemed to save her mothering for the people she cared most for, with Rebecca in the fore-front.

"About time you got here," Max snapped, breaking her reverie.

Laura froze as the thundering of hooves came toward them and the loud crack of a mallet hitting a wooden ball vibrated in the still, cold air. She picked Houston out quickly. In the powder-blue jersey with the number three on the back, he was riding in the middle of the pack.

He shouted to another player, who wheeled to intercept the ball. In a flash, the whole pack had changed direction and was riding at top speed.

Laura remembered enough from her childhood to know that Houston would be directing the team from the number-three spot, which was the usual position for the team's strongest player, and mainly defensive. The number-two position would be the main scorer, backed by the number one. And the back, who wore the number four, would be the main defender.

By the time she had gotten the players sorted out, the teams had traveled the field twice, with the Sta-

tion team scoring early in the first chukker. Catching
the animated spirit of the afternoon, she leaned forward in her chair and clapped enthusiastically along
with everyone else.

Realizing what she had done, Laura glanced to the
side and found Julia watching her with a smile.

Jessy leaned across Rebecca and said, "You've got
to admit, it's not a dull game."

"No," Laura answered, wondering if everyone had
been looking at her, "it's not a dull game."

Jessy beamed at her and patted her hand encour-
agingly, and Laura knew that she had been added to
Jessy's select list of people to watch over. After
spending her whole life taking care of other people,
Laura was finding it difficult getting used to so many
people suddenly trying to take care of her. First
Houston, then her mother and now Houston's sisters
seemed to be adopting her. It was nice, but she was
afraid she was in danger of being spoiled.

The heavy breathing of horses accompanied the
pounding of hooves, and she looked up in time to see
a clash just yards in front of her. A player on the op-
posing Rawlson team rode his pony roughly into the
side of the Station's back in an attempt to reach the
ball. Another Rawlson player rode across the front
and picked up the ball with a resounding whack, and
the riders thundered past in pursuit.

Laura tensed then forced herself to relax. No one
had been hurt. No one had even been in danger. Polo
was a rough game, and everyone who played was capable of staying in the saddle through a little bout of

bumping. Besides, Houston hadn't been anywhere near the ball.

She took a deep breath and glanced to the side to find Rebecca waiting to give her an encouraging smile.

"It always makes my heart pound a little faster when they collide like that," Rebecca confessed. "But they never seem to pay any attention when it happens, so I try not to worry."

Laura nodded. "I guess that's about all we can do." She knew Houston had told them to take care of her, but she was beginning to feel as if she had three baby-sitters for the afternoon, and it really wasn't necessary.

At the other end of the field Houston took control of the ball, sent it whizzing toward the number-one member of their team, then rode hell-bent toward the Station goal with the rest of the players in pursuit. Crisscrossing the field, they managed to keep the Rawlson team from reaching the ball while Houston and the number one and two players passed the ball until Houston hit a scoring shot.

Laura jumped to her feet, cheering wildly. She had always known he had the combination of horsemanship, athletic ability and aggression that it took to be a good player. What she hadn't known was that she would enjoy watching him so intensely.

She felt pride and love rising inside her. The way he sat on his horse, looking so tall and graceful in the saddle. The way he looked in his uniform, with the tight blue polo shirt and the tight white pants and the knee-high brown boots, the first nice-looking pair of boots she had seen him in. She was a little shocked to find herself thinking how wonderfully masculine he looked.

She realized her reaction was the sort that bare, sweat-slick muscles and sizzlingly hot summer days have been known to produce, but she had never thought she was the sort of woman who would feel that way. And here she was, practically panting over her fiancé, having barely controllable libidinous visions and wondering how much longer it would be before this blasted game was over.

"Isn't he wonderful?" Jessy cried, reaching over Rebecca again to clasp Laura's hand.

"Yes, he is," Laura replied without taking her eyes from the man of her dreams. Heading to the pony line at the end of the chukker, he rode near and tipped his helmet to her with a broad smile. She applauded and blew him a kiss before he rode away.

Max cleared his throat loudly, and Laura turned to look at him on the other side of her mother. "It looks like you may live through this after all," he said when he had her attention. "It looks like you may even be enjoying yourself."

"Well," Laura said, still smiling, "I'm ashamed to admit it, but I think I'm beginning to have a little fun."

"He's a damned good player, you know."

"So were you, Dad. That was never the problem," Laura said, sobering.

"It's a lovely day, isn't it?" Julia asked no one in particular. "It's definitely winter, but the sun's very warm and there's no wind to speak of. I don't mind winter at all when it's this civilized."

Laura almost laughed. Her mother really was a jewel. "I agree totally," she said, holding herself to a smile. "I think this has been a very lovely and civilized winter so far."

"Of course, we're probably going to have a wet spring," Julia continued, "since it's rained so little this winter."

"What do you think, Rebecca?" Laura asked, turning to her other side.

"Well, I was just thinking of taking off my coat, since it's such a lovely, sunny day. I'm getting warm sitting here all bundled up," Rebecca answered with a straight face.

"Don't you dare," Jessy said. "You can't get sick for another five months."

"Oh, look," Rebecca said, pointing to the field.

The game had begun again, and the eight players were once again racing pell-mell past them. The shouts of the riders blended with the thunder of hooves and the crack of wood striking wood. The frightening thud of horse colliding with horse added to the tense excitement of a rough, hard-fought game.

"I don't think I like that rider very much," Julia said quietly. "He seems to spend more time running into other riders than he does going after the ball. Do you know him, Max?"

"He's a local boy. He's got more enthusiasm than sense, but he's harmless."

"He's certainly not very graceful."

"This is polo, Julia, not ballet."

"Look," Rebecca said, "Houston's taking another shot."

Laura turned her attention from her parents to the field and quickly identified Houston. Standing in the stirrups, he lifted the mallet behind him then brought it down in a sweeping forward swing. He leaned low and to the side, then rose on the follow-through as the ball darted across the field to a forward player.

Wheeling to avoid another player, he pointed his sure-footed pony in the direction of the action. Laura smiled as she watched him running interference then magically merging with the path of the ball to take another graceful roundhouse swing and send the ball careening toward the goal. Changing direction and speed, he rode with the other players, blocking and aiding until the Station team scored.

The excitement of the onlookers had built with the pace of the game. The polite applause of the first chukker had given way to indiscriminate cheers each time a goal was made. The game had been unexpectedly fast-paced and high-scoring, and Laura couldn't help thinking that Houston had been a big part of it.

He really was good. He looked at home on horseback. She sighed and realized that she might as well face the fact that he just wasn't the lounge-chair type. Put him on a horse and stick a mallet in his hand and he became electrified. If she was selfish enough to ask him to give it up, and if he loved her enough to comply, she wouldn't be winning anything, and he would be losing a lot. And she loved him too much to ask.

"You look lost in thought," Julia said quietly.

"I was." Laura looked at her and smiled. "I was thinking what a terrific mother you are and that I should listen to you more often."

"Well, thank you. What wonderful thing did I do this time?"

"You talked me into this." She spread her hands to encompass her surroundings. "And I think you gave me a much happier marriage than I would have had otherwise."

"Experience, dear." Julia took her hand and squeezed gently. "Sometimes it helps to talk to someone who's made the mistakes before you."

With her new attitude in place, Laura turned toward the field to locate Houston. On the far side, the players were in a tight knot that seemed to be circling sideways in a jostling, jockeying mass. Suddenly a player broke free, and one by one the others followed him.

Straining to see into the midst of the pack, Laura made out the number three on the blue shirt. Riding full speed, Houston appeared to be in a stick fight with another player. Houston knocked the ball forward. The other player knocked it in front of Houston's horse. In a reaching move that was blatantly illegal, the Rawlson player drove his horse into the side of Houston's pony and tangled his stick in the legs of Houston's mount.

Laura sucked in her breath in a moan and rose to her feet as she watched Houston's horse stumble forward. Houston shifted his weight in the saddle and pulled on the reins, fighting to keep the horse up. Like a low roar around her she could hear the crowd's reaction.

Almost in slow motion, the horse went to his knees, pitching Houston forward. The pony skidded and began to lean to the side. At the last minute, Houston jumped free, rolling as he landed, and for an instant Laura lost sight of him among the horses' hooves.

The people around her echoed her shocked gasp and rose to their feet while she strained to find Houston. Confused shouts from the playing field carried across the ground. The riders pulled up, circled back and reined in. One pony, unable to stop, leaped over the small, dark mound that was Houston.

A hush fell as they waited for the fallen rider to move.

"Oh, God, no," Laura cried. It was happening again. It was all happening again. Without thinking, she ran toward the field, only to be restrained by faceless arms that reached out to hold her.

"Let me go!" she shouted, and shoved at the hands that clasped her.

"It's too dangerous for you to go out there," a strong male voice answered. "Look, he's up."

In her panic she had trouble focusing. "Where?"

"It's all right, baby. He's up. He's okay," her mother said, and gently folded Laura into her arms.

Tears of relief filled her eyes. "Damn it, I can't see," Laura said, wiping angrily at the sudden tears.

When she had cleared her vision, she watched Houston run his hands slowly over the legs of his mount before swinging himself into the saddle again. He raised his arms to the crowd, signaling that he was all right, and the crowd broke into a grateful applause.

"See, hon, he's just fine," Julia said.

Her tears still flowing, Laura turned her frustrated anger on her mother. "Just fine? He could have been killed." She jerked free of the consoling arms that still held her. "And you want to know the worst part? I was enjoying it. I was proud of him."

"Laura..." Julia reached out to her, but Laura backed away.

"It'll never be all right." She caught her breath in a sob as her mother's image rippled in a sea of tears. "Never. And I was a fool to think it would."

Other hands brushed against her. Soft hands. Caring hands. But she didn't want anyone's sympathy. Her world was in ruins. Her heart was broken. She had tried to put the past behind her, but the ghosts wouldn't let her. They rose to haunt her. Laura kept backing away, feeling trapped by everyone's well-meaning concern. She had to get away. She had to be alone with the terrible ache that was eating at her. She had to stop the pictures that kept replaying in her mind.

"Laura!"

Her mother's voice followed her, and Laura held up a hand. "Not now," she whispered. "Please, let me go. I have to go." And she turned and ran.

Bells were still ringing softly in Houston's head, but nothing was broken. As he waved to the crowd, he looked for Laura, but people seemed to be moving, leaning over, talking to their neighbors, stretching. There seemed to be nothing better than a close call to wake up a crowd.

Finally he saw Max in his wheelchair, smiling as he watched something in the distance. Next to him was an empty chair, the chair Julia had been in, and next to that was an overturned chair. Next he saw Rebecca. Her hand at her throat, she was staring in dismay toward the parking area, the same direction Max had been facing. Beside her, Jessy was a picture of worry, turning from the parking area to Rebecca and back again, unable to decide which one needed her attention most.

A dark premonition began gnawing at him as he scanned the crowd. In the foreground he found Julia, standing alone, with her hands on her hips. While he watched, she stalked toward Max with body language that clearly spelled anger.

Unaware of her, Max continued to smile into the distance. Looking more closely, Houston could see cold satisfaction in the smile. "Oh, God, no," he said. A shudder ran down his back, followed by a sudden hot flash of anger. Almost afraid to look, he turned toward the parking area in time to see Laura's red convertible heading toward the gate in a flurry of plowed turf and flying gravel.

Rage and self-incrimination screamed inside him. Almost in tears, he whirled his horse in a circle, first toward the parked cars, then toward the pony line where the horse trailers were, and where his car should have been. But he had ridden with the horses. He didn't have a car, and he could never catch her on horseback, even if his horse was sound enough to gallop to the main house after its fall.

"Houston! Houston!"

He turned to the crowd and saw Jessy running toward the field, waving something in her hand. Wonderful Jessy, Houston thought, spurring his horse to meet her. She was possibly the only one in the family more impetuous than he was, but she was superb in a crisis. He reined to a halt and reached down to take the keys she was thrusting at him.

"Rebecca's car." She pointed in the direction Laura had gone. "Go. Hurry."

"I love you," Houston shouted as he headed toward Rebecca's car.

"She was really upset," Jessy called after him. "Good luck."

When he was on the road to the main house, Houston's mind finally slowed down enough for him to realize that Max must have been hoping for just the sort of thing that happened. He had picked the players on the Station team. He had known the sort of fast, rough game the Rawlson team favored. He had set the whole thing up to break up their engagement, not to celebrate it.

And like a fool, Houston had walked into the trap. He could have slowed the game down. He could have been more cautious. But like a stupid teenager, he had been showing off for the woman he loved, trying to impress her with his dashing horsemanship.

Instead, he had fallen on his face and scared her to death. It wasn't enough that she'd had to go through it with her father. He'd made her relive it, knowing it was the one thing she couldn't take.

"Damn!" he said aloud, and pounded his fist on the steering wheel. He should have been mad at Max, but he was too mad at himself to have any anger left for anyone else. All he could feel for Max was sorrow. He was a lonely, embittered old man, too threatened by the happiness of others to have any happiness in his own life.

There was a time when Houston had thought of Max almost as a second father, and he had thought Max felt like a father to him. It hurt to know that he had lost Max as a friend, but it didn't hurt nearly as much as it would if he lost Laura.

Skidding to a halt in front of the house, he left the keys in the car and ran across the terrace and into the foyer.

Etta looked up from her vacuuming and shut off the motor when she saw Houston. "I knew it was something bad," she said, shaking her head.

"Where is she?"

She nodded her head toward the stairs. "In her room. But the door's locked and she won't talk."

"Have you got a key?"

Etta put on her stubborn face. "She's a grown woman. And if she doesn't open that door herself, it's not going to open."

Houston took a deep breath and tried to calm down. Already his body was getting stiff from the fall. A headache throbbed dully at the base of his skull. "You're right."

He walked to the staircase and took the stairs one at a time, preparing himself to beg, plead and promise anything he had to. If she never wanted him on a horse again, he could live with it. The one thing he couldn't live without was her. If she wanted humility, he was humbled. If she needed his patience, he would be patient. He would be understanding. He would be anything she wanted. Anything.

At her door, his nerves got the best of him and his knock was harder and louder than he intended. It sounded angry and demanding.

"Laura?" he said softly, trying to make up for the knock. "Honey, it's me." He listened and heard nothing but silence. "Baby, I'm so sorry. Can we talk? Oh, Laura," he whispered, and leaned his head against the door. An almost overwhelming urge to cry swept over him. The last thing in the world he had wanted to do was to hurt her, but that was exactly what he had done.

He had known from the beginning that he would have to go slowly and treat her with care. He had known she carried old wounds that would take time to heal, and yet he had rushed her. He had promised her nothing but happiness, and he had given her nightmares.

Slowly the door opened, and he lifted his head to find Laura watching him from barely a foot away.

"It wasn't locked," she said softly.

She had been crying, and his heart broke a little to see the tear stains on her cheeks. "Etta said it was." He gestured vaguely toward the stairs.

"I saw you drive up."

She had unlocked it for him. She wanted to see him. He would have smiled, but there was still too much pain in her eyes for him to celebrate.

"Could I come in?" he asked.

Laura moved and let him in. Then she closed the door.

"Are you all right?" she asked, leading him to the love seat in the corner.

"Bumps and bruises. They should work themselves out in a day or so."

"And the horse?"

"He seemed to be fine. They'll have a vet look him over just to be sure."

She nodded and tried to smile, and they sat in silence while he watched her nervously slide her engagement ring on and off her finger. Houston had the uncomfortable feeling that her actions unconsciously mirrored her thoughts. The ring seemed to get farther off her finger with each slide, and when he couldn't take it anymore, he reached over and took her hand, putting the ring firmly in place.

"Whatever happened today," he said, "we can fix it."

"Oh, Houston." She stared at him with misery on her face and tears welling in her eyes.

"I'll quit polo. I'll do anything."

"No. You can't. It wouldn't be right." The tears spilled over and trailed down her cheeks. "I couldn't ask that. It's just . . ."

She broke down totally and hid her face in a tissue she pulled from the packet she carried with her.

Houston put his arms around her and pulled her against his chest. "Oh, Laura, honey, baby, please. Ask it. I'll do it. I'll do anything." He patted her and tried not to sound as panicked as he felt. "Just, please, honey, please don't cry anymore. You don't know what it does to me. I just can't stand it.''

"I love you, Houston," she sobbed. "I really, really love you. But I just don't know if it's enough."

"It's enough. We'll make it enough. I'll make it enough."

"I just hurt so bad. And I'm sorry. I know this isn't your fault."

"Yes, it is," he argued urgently. "I was showing off for you, Laura. I was trying to impress you. It's all my fault."

"No." She shook her head and tossed the tissue into a wastebasket at the side of the love seat, then pulled a new tissue from the packet. "It's not your fault. It's not even the polo. It's just everything. I'm so confused."

"What do you mean?"

She dried her eyes and dabbed at her cheeks and made a valiant attempt to look at him calmly. "You impressed me. I enjoyed the match, and I finally understood how much you must enjoy playing. You even..." She paused, and a blush crept charmingly up her neck.

"I even?" Houston prompted. He had been fighting the urge to kiss her since he had entered the room.

"Well, watching you play, sort of..."

She stalled again, and the blush grew a deeper shade of pink. Maintaining his control was a sweet torture as she ducked her head to hide her embarrassment.

Houston curled his finger under her chin and gently lifted her head. "Yes?" he asked.

"It was sort of a turn-on," she said softly, breathlessly.

He laughed and found himself enjoying the idea immensely. "Really?"

She lowered her head and looked at him through her eyelashes. Her cheeks were red. "Really."

He met his impulse halfway and kissed her temple, hugging her gently. "Does that embarrass you?"

"Well, it didn't then. But..." She sighed, and he could feel her sag in his arms.

"But then the accident spoiled it," he finished for her.

"I love you. But I'm so confused. I need time, Houston. Time to sort out what I'm feeling."

"How much time?"

"I don't know. The apartment's ready. I think I'm going to go ahead and move in."

His heart sank. He didn't want her so far away. He didn't want her to get used to being without him.

"Do you want me to give this back?" she asked, holding out the ring she had taken off her finger.

In anger and despair, Houston took the ring and put it on her finger. "Don't do that," he said harshly. Then he forced himself to draw in a slow, calm breath, and he said quietly, "Please, don't do that. We'll work this out, Laura. Whatever it takes, however long it takes, we'll work this out."

"But the wedding..."

"It's still almost two months away. And if that's not enough time, we'll postpone it."

She rubbed her hand over her forehead. "I'm tired. I'm just so tired."

He held her close. He heard the fatigue in her voice and wished he could help her somehow. But all he could do was wait and be there for her when she needed him. Eventually she would realize the part Max had played, and her pain would be stronger than the loss Houston felt.

He stayed with her until she fell asleep in his arms. Then he carried her to her bed and covered her with a quilt. Downstairs the families gathered in the living room, held at bay by Etta until Houston arrived. With a wink and a nod, Etta turned the assembly over to him and returned to her housework.

"She's asleep," Houston said simply.

Jessy and Rebecca said nothing, but from the sympathy in their eyes he knew they understood the battle wasn't won.

"Do you think she'll sleep for a while?" Julia asked.

From the distance she kept from Max, Houston assumed that her anger was still intact.

"She seemed pretty exhausted."

"Then I guess we'll just leave her alone. I hate to ask, but..." She raised her brows in a question, hesitant to say the words aloud.

"The wedding date is unchanged for now, but the wedding is on hold." His stomach was in knots. If he had been alone, he might have given in to the despair he had been battling since his spill. It took all his strength to go on. "She's moving into the apartment in Savannah while she decides what she's going to do."

Jessy and Rebecca remained silent. Bitterness bordering on hatred boiled inside him. He despised himself for feeling it, but it was there nevertheless, and there seemed to be nothing he could do about it at the moment.

He looked at Max, expecting to find him gloating, but there was no satisfaction on the other man's face now. Taking Houston's silence as a signal, Rebecca and Jessy stood and almost tiptoed from the room. Julia followed them, bravely touching Houston's arm in parting, and he found the gesture surprisingly comforting, perhaps because he could see so much of the daughter in the mother.

When they were alone, Houston stood watching Max, looking for the triumph he had seen earlier. Surely Max wasn't afraid of him. No matter how angry he was, he would never stoop to physical violence with a man in a wheelchair.

"I had expected to feel happier," Max said finally.

"You looked pretty damned happy right after it happened."

"It didn't last. I guess they're right about revenge. It isn't what you think it's going to be."

Damn the man. "Max, if you're going to be a sneaky little bastard and pull something like this, the least you could do is remain a sneaky little bastard when it's over."

Max shook his head. "I was wrong. I shouldn't have done it. I'm not going to ask you to forgive me, but I will talk to Laura and try to right the wrong I've done to you both."

In a flash, Houston's anger was back. "No, you won't. She's been through enough, and the last thing she needs to know right now is that her father did it to her on purpose. You're not going to say one word to Laura."

"It's better for her to be mad at me than at you," Max argued.

"Not one word," Houston said. "And if you do, I swear I'll find a way to make you sorry." It was just like the stubborn old goat to be arrogant and headstrong about his own guilt.

Defiance flashed in Max's eyes. "The estate, then," he said, determined to make amends on his own terms. "Forget the sale. I'll give it to you as a wedding present."

Houston felt his anger boiling over. "Max," he said through gritted teeth, "you can take this farm and shove it. Without Laura, I don't want it."

"I'll sell it to someone else, then."

"No, you won't. Because it's still half Julia's. You can't sell it without her consent. And she's not going to give you her consent, because she's more disgusted with you than I am."

"Look, I'm sorry. What do I have to do?"

Anger, hurt and a sense of devastating loss weighed on Houston. Not just his loss, but everyone's loss, and the worst part was that none of it had to have happened.

"I don't know, Max," he began, saying what was in his heart. "Maybe you have to learn how to be a human being again. Maybe you have to learn to stop beating up on everybody else because life dealt you a low blow. You have two daughters who would have given anything to love you the way they should have been able to love their father. You have a beautiful wife who obviously still cares about you, or she would have divorced you and found somebody else a long time ago. You have a lot, Max. You have more than I may ever have.''

Chapter Twelve

Laura sat on the edge of the sofa, staring at the papers scattered across the coffee table. Her grand opening was barely two months away, and there was still much to do.

"Here you go," Rebecca said, and handed her a cup of tea.

"Oh, thanks." She sniffed the steaming tea as Rebecca settled into a chair next to her. "At least I'll be able to say that every tea I sell has been personally tested," she said, laughing.

"The tea, I don't mind," Rebecca answered. "But if you don't stop trying out new recipes on me, I'm going to be as big as a blimp."

"All blimps should look so good."

At five months, Rebecca's tall, slender frame barely showed the effects of her pregnancy, and the sadness that had seemed so much a part of her just a few months earlier was all but gone.

"Seriously," Laura said, "I don't know what I would have done without you this past month. You've been such a help. Are you sure you won't stay after the baby comes? I could really use you."

"It's tempting, Laura." Rebecca tucked her legs under her and sipped at the steaming tea. "Ooh, I like this one. I think it'll be a good seller," she said, referring to the latest flavor they were sampling. "Anyway, my grandfather left me some land in West Texas. It's not really good for much, but I'm thinking of spending some time there."

"Well, if you ever change your mind, you're worth your weight in gold as far as I'm concerned," Laura said, glancing at the balloon curtains Rebecca had made for the three long windows in the apartment. She had also made a set for the windows in the tearoom and some for the shop. She'd been a second pair of legs for Laura on countless errands. She'd re-covered the sofa that Laura had picked up at a garage sale and had made matching lamp shades for the lamps Laura had bought at an auction.

She'd served as decorator, adviser and friend, and Laura was going to miss her when she was gone.

"I'm really going to hate to see you leave. But Texas is your home," she said, trying not to sound as sad as she felt. She couldn't help remembering that the same was true of Houston, and that when the renovations were done, he might be leaving, as well.

A tentative knock on the open door behind her interrupted her thoughts. Laura looked over her shoulder and saw Tony in the doorway. Construction had progressed much faster once the third story entrance level with Bay Street had been opened. At this stage there was so much going on that people were in and out all day, and at night, when the sounds of hammers and saws had ceased, the silence echoed.

"Uh, Miss Warner," Tony said hesitantly, "Houston wants you downstairs, ma'am, double quick."

"Double quick?" Laura asked, raising her eyebrows.

"Uh, he told me to say that, ma'am."

"I'll be right there, Tony. Thank you." She turned to Rebecca and rolled her eyes. "Ma'am. I'm in the prime of my life, and he makes me feel so old."

"He's working on a business you're going to own. It's a sign of respect." Rebecca grinned. "And you probably intimidate him, Miss Warner, ma'am."

"You!" Laura said, laughing. "You're so much like your brother."

Rebecca held up her hands innocently. "I'm staying out of that one. I'm sitting right here. I don't even want to be in the same room with you two."

"We're not that bad, are we?"

"He looks at you when you're not looking. You look at him when he's not looking. It's painful, Laura. You two are so miserable, but..." She held up her hands again. "It's none of my business."

"I should decide, shouldn't I?"

"Or figure out why you keep putting it off."

Laura bit her lip and nodded. "Yeah. You're right. I should do that." Then she took a deep breath and spread a smile across her face. "I guess I'd better go. I'm not being very double quick."

All the way down the stairs her heart pounded. She wanted to see him, and she didn't want to see him. She wanted to be with him, and she didn't want to be with him. She wanted to make up her mind, and she didn't want to, because she was as terrified as anyone of the decision she would make, and as long as she was undecided, she still had him.

The coffee shop was empty when she got there. No workers, no Houston, no nothing. "Houston?"

"Back here."

She followed the sound of his voice to the second room of the shop, the room that would open last, and she found him waiting in the center of the room.

"Hi," she said uncertainly, looking around for someone else. There was no one to be found.

"Hi."

"You sent for me?"

He nodded, turned and walked to the other side of the room, and Laura knew it was going to be bad news. When he couldn't look at her, it was never good.

"How are you doing?" he asked, turning slowly.

"How am I doing?"

He nodded. "Really doing. I know you're keeping busy during the day, but how are the nights?"

"Oh." It was a personal talk. They hadn't had one of those in a while. They hadn't even been alone in a while, and she was beginning to realize why. She was lonely. She was miserable, and if she tried to tell him so, she'd probably break down and cry.

"Well, there's plenty to do at night," she said carefully. "But the nights can still get pretty long."

"Pretty long, huh?" He turned and paced again. "Well, I'll tell you how my nights are." He leaned his shoulder against the wall and looked at her from a three-quarter profile. "They're hell. And my days aren't much better. I've been waiting a month for some sign from you, and all I can see you doing is getting farther away from me."

"You said—"

"I said I'd give you all the time you needed, and I'm sorry. In a little less than a month we're supposed to be getting married. And I think if I don't know something soon, I'm going to go out of my mind."

For the past month she had avoided looking directly at Houston as much as she could. Now, alone with him, she couldn't seem to look anywhere else. And what she saw hurt. His beautiful blue eyes were rimmed with red. His cheeks were hollower and his clothes were looser. He seemed tired and on edge.

He looked like a man who was at his limit, and she knew that if she couldn't give him an answer soon, he would give her one. "I understand," she said. The weekend was just a few days away. It would be quiet then. She could think. "Would this weekend be all right?"

"Saturday."

She nodded. "Saturday." She stood there while he walked past.

When he was behind her, he stopped and touched her shoulder. "I'm sorry. I just can't go on this way any longer."

Without turning, she put her hand over his. "I
know."

He left, and she went on standing there with tears
streaming down her cheeks.

A breeze blew in from the balcony and across the
bare wood floor of the empty tearoom. Sunbeams
streamed through the three tall windows that over-
looked the river, and dust motes danced inside the
golden shafts of light. Drawn by the hint of spring that
warmed the air, Laura walked through one of the
ceiling-high windows onto the balcony.

Her hands on the railing, she studied the river and
tried to recapture the sense of elation she had once
had. She had been living in her apartment for over a
month. The renovations were almost done on the
business. This was supposed to be a happy time. This
was supposed to be the secure future that was all she
really wanted.

But standing alone in that bare room, the only future she could see looked cold and empty. It might be
a safe, secure future, but it was a lonely one, and she
was tired of being lonely.

"Laura? Dear? Where are you?"

Laura turned and went into the restaurant.
"Mother? I'm in here."

Max came through the door first, with Julia following. "Are you surprised?" Julia asked, smiling.

Laura had hardly been to the farm since she had
moved out, and Max seldom left it, so they had seen
little of each other since the polo match, and she
wasn't sure she was entirely happy to see him now.

"Actually, yes, I am," she said slowly. It was Saturday. She had been expecting Houston. Having someone else arrive was a little disconcerting, and watching her mother nervously toy with her handkerchief was more than a little disconcerting.

Suddenly Laura was afraid. Houston had made his decision. He was gone. Her mother had come to hold her hand, and her father had come to gloat. "What is it?" she asked in a breathless voice that had lost its strength.

Julia smiled almost blissfully. Max blushed, and Laura frowned. It couldn't be about Houston. Her mother was happy and her father was . . . shy? "What is it?" she said again, suspiciously.

"Well," Julia said, and reached out to take the hand Max offered her. She held his hand tightly in both of hers and started again. Her cheeks were a delicate shade of rose. "Your father and I . . ."

Julia blushed furiously and stammered to a halt. Laura's eyes filled with tears, and she fumbled in the pockets of her jeans for the packet of tissues she was never without these days. Now, of all times. After all the years she had wasted hoping and wishing and dreaming that her parents would get back together, they had waited until she was in the middle of the biggest crisis of her life, and then they did it.

"What your mother is trying to say is that she's not going back to Arkansas," Max said, his gruff voice softer than it had been in fourteen years.

"What your mother is trying to say," Julia added, "is that she's home for good."

Laura drew in a ragged breath and buried her face in her tissue and sobbed. She was happy. She was very happy, but it had been a long, hard week at the end of a long, hard month. All her dreams were coming true at once, and they weren't enough anymore.

Without Houston, nothing mattered as much as it used to. Without Houston, nothing was really very important.

Her tears stopped when an arm that was much too strong to be her mother's went around Laura's shoulders and pulled her against a chest that was definitely not her mother's. Opening her eyes, she saw Houston's face above hers.

"We sort of expected you to be happy with the news," he said.

"I am happy," Laura mumbled through the tissue. She peeked around his shoulder and saw that her mother and father were gone. "Where did they go?"

"Well, you were so happy, they thought maybe you should be alone for a while."

She looked at him and frowned. He was relaxed. The red rims around his eyes were gone. He was still thin, but he had the look of a man who had eaten one of Etta's breakfasts and enjoyed it. And Laura couldn't help being worried.

"I'm sorry about the other day," he said.

"What?"

"The ultimatum. I shouldn't have done that. I promised you all the time you needed, and I guess if I have to spend the rest of my life just being engaged, that's better than nothing. Unless, of course, you've made up your mind. Have you?"

"Well, yes, I think I have. But wait a minute." She held up her hand. "Are you saying now that I don't have to?"

Houston rolled his eyes to the heavens and clenched his fists at his sides. "Laura," he said through gritted teeth.

All his patience disappeared. The man on edge was back, and she had to bite her lip to keep from smiling.

Houston turned and paced toward the door. Just as Laura said, "Wait!" he turned and started toward her.

"You drive me crazy sometimes," he said as if she hadn't said a thing. "I love you, Laura." He swept her into his arms. "I love you so much."

He kissed her for the first time in a month, and Laura felt her bones melt from the heat of the volcano that erupted inside her. His hands clenched and unclenched on her back. His mouth twisted on hers. His tongue slipped between her lips, touching her tongue, circling and withdrawing. His hands slid lower, caressing her rounded derriere and pulling her against him with a grinding force that sent a shuddering groan through her.

He pulled his mouth from hers and whispered against her lips, "Marry me, Laura."

"Oh, yes," she gasped. It had been a month since he had touched her.

He lifted his face and looked into her eyes. "Do you mean it?"

"Yes." She had just been fooling herself thinking she could ever live without him. If he had only kissed her sooner, it would never have taken her so long to make up her mind.

"When did you decide?" he asked warily. He loosened his grip and put some space between them. "I don't want you to make any promises in the heat of the moment that you can't stick to later."

"Oh, Houston." She breathed his name like a caress. "You're the most important thing in my life. What good does all this do me without you?" She waved her arm at the renovations that surrounded them. "Nothing's any good when you're all alone. And when you're not with the person you love, you're always alone. And I'm so tired of being alone."

He pulled her close again. "Are you sure?"

"There's not a doubt in my mind. Not anymore."

"And..." He stopped as a new worry crossed his face.

Reading his mind, Laura touched Houston's cheek and kissed him gently on the lips. Then she looked into his eyes. "If I could wrap you in cotton and keep you safe forever, I would. But I can't. And I won't ask you to change what you are or give up the things you love."

"I would, if you ever wanted me to. There's only one thing I can't live without," he said with feeling, "and that's you."

Laura smiled, a sudden, unbearable happiness gripping her, and she moved into his waiting arms. "Just don't fall off your horse again," she murmured contentedly.

His lips brushed her temples. "I could say the same thing to you."

She nestled against his chest and drank in the feel of him after a long drought. "I guess we'll just have to learn to live with it," she said, snuggling closer.

"I guess we will," he answered as he tightened his embrace.

Houston's mouth grazed hers. Then he kissed her again, seriously, slowly and deeply, with a hunger that would last a lifetime, and the slanting rays of the sun moved slowly across the floor, growing longer and paler.

* * * * *

Silhouette Special Edition

COMING NEXT MONTH

#607 BEST MAN—Jo Ann Algermissen
Sylas Kincaid detected the pain masked by Alana Benton's brittle poise, and he sensed that masculine cruelty had put it there. But surely the love of a better man would bring her heart out of hiding...

#608 A WOMAN'S WORK—Laura Leone
Hardworking Marla Foster stunned her firm by capturing Brent Ventura's account. But Brent's dangerously unprofessional mix of irreverence and relentless sex appeal soon proved Marla's job had only just begun!

#609 THE OTHER MOTHER—Pamela Jerrold
Her suddenly widowed sister left pregnant surrogate mother Caitlin O'Shea high and dry. But prodigal brother-in-law Sam Ellison seemed oddly eager to keep Caitlin's bundle of joy all in the family.

#610 MY FIRST LOVE, MY LAST—Pat Warren
Rafe Sloan's motives for helping Nora Maddox find her missing son weren't entirely altruistic. The abrupt ending to their old affair had left burning questions, and Rafe was prepared to probe deeply for the answers....

#611 WITH NO REGRETS—Lisa Jackson
Jaded attorney Jake McGowan rationalized that he was helping beautiful, desperate Kimberly Bennett with her child-custody suit merely to win *him* sweet revenge on Kimberly's shady ex-husband. So why was his trademark cynicism beginning to feel like caring?

#612 WALK UPON THE WIND—Christine Flynn
A hurricane blew sheltered Nicole Stewart into Aaron Wilde's untamed world. Their island idyll couldn't last, but could she return to privileged society once she'd tasted primitive passion, once she'd walked upon the wind?

AVAILABLE THIS MONTH:

Silhouette Romance®

CIMARRON STORIES

A TRILOGY BY PEPPER ADAMS

Pepper Adams is back and spicier than ever with three tender, heartwarming tales, set on the plains of Oklahoma.

CIMARRON KNIGHT ... available in June
Rugged rancher and dyed-in-the-wool bachelor Brody Sawyer meets his match in determined Noelle Chandler and her adorable twin boys!

CIMARRON GLORY ... available in August
With a stubborn streak as strong as her foster brother Brody's, Glory Roberts has her heart set on lassoing handsome loner Ross Forbes ... and uncovering his mysterious past....

CIMARRON REBEL ... available in October
Brody's brother Riley is a handsome rebel with a cause! And he doesn't mind getting roped into marrying Darcy Durant—in name only—to gain custody of two heartbroken kids.

**Don't miss CIMARRON KNIGHT, CIMARRON GLORY and
CIMARRON REBEL—three special stories that'll win your
heart ... available only from Silhouette Romance!**

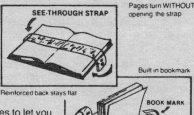

A BIG SISTER
can take her places

She likes that. Her Mom does too.

BIG BROTHERS/BIG SISTERS AND HARLEQUIN

Harlequin is proud to announce its official sponsorship of Big Brothers/Big Sisters of America. Look for this poster in your local Big Brothers/Big Sisters agency or call them to get one in your favorite bookstore. Love is all about sharing.

BB/BS-1A